Steel Tracks - Iron Men

After recovering from a shoulder wound received during the bloody war against a rival railroad company, Cole Shand is plunged into action even before he can report for duty in Longhorn Crossing.

As boss-man of the South-West Railroad trouble-shooters, locked in a grim battle for supremacy with the unscrupulous owners of the Harvey Thompson Railroad, Shand had thought that the fighting could not get any worse.

But when ruthless killers are employed by his enemies to accomplish their greedy aims, Shand knows he will have to fight until the last bitter shot.

Steel Tracks - Iron Men

CORBA SUNMAN

A Black Horse Western

ROBERT HALE · LONDON

© Corba Sunman 2006
First published in Great Britain 2006

ISBN-10: 0-7090-7892-7
ISBN-13: 978-0-7090-7892-0

Robert Hale Limited
Clerkenwell House
Clerkenwell Green
London EC1R 0HT

Typeset by Derek Doyle & Associates, Shaw Heath.
Printed and bound in Great Britain by
Antony Rowe Limited, Wiltshire.

ONE

Cole Shand sighed impatiently as he eased his powerful body on the hard seat of the smooth-running train making its way towards Longhorn Crossing in New Mexico. He knew every mile of the interminable trip, having supervised the troubleshooting section of SWRR for the past five years, and this southern fork of the mighty railroad was pushing west towards Indian Pass: the gateway to California lying beyond.

Shand massaged his left shoulder gingerly. It had not fully recovered from the bullet wound he received in the showdown that had smashed the organized resistance of the competitors to South-West Rail Road's bid to be the first company to lay tracks through Indian Pass in the High Sierra Mountains. The Harvey Thompson Railroad Company – HTR – had employed gunslingers and saboteurs in a mean and dirty fight to beat SWRR to Indian Pass – the first to reach the pass would be rewarded with the franchise to lay tracks all the way to California.

Aged twenty-six, blue-eyed and yellow-haired,

Shand was over six feet tall, and his grey store suit failed to conceal the powerful lines of his tough, well-muscled body. His lean, angular face showed signs of his way of life – a two-inch white scar through his left eyebrow and another on the right side of his pugnacious chin. He was wearing a grey Stetson and black store shoes. A dark-leather cartridge belt encircled his slim waist, its loops filled with gleaming .45 shells for the Colt revolver nestling in the tied-down holster on his right thigh.

Shand tried to relax. While he had been recovering from his wound in El Paso there had been no word of more trouble hitting the railroad. In the bloody showdown, his band of troubleshooters had routed HTR's gang of renegades and he had personally arrested Nat Poggin, the hardcase who had been bossing HTR's campaign of dirty tricks. All reports since the showdown indicated that the work of pushing SWRR tracks south and west was progressing smoothly – too smoothly, Shand suspected, for he felt certain that HTR had not given up the fight for the franchise.

During his convalescence Shand had been beset by thoughts of what had gone before, and his attitude towards the rival railroad company had hardened to the extent that he was eager now to lead his troubleshooting crew to HTR's end of track and to obliterate their construction camp to put them out of the race to Indian Pass.

He settled in his seat, tilted his broad-brimmed Stetson forward over his pale eyes, and tried to relax. There was time enough to resume the harness of troubleshooting when he reached Longhorn Crossing, where Frank Merrick, the district superintendent, was located. He drifted into an uneasy sleep, but was jerked awake almost immediately by an insistent hand shaking his shoulder. He opened his eyes to find Mike O'Toole, the conductor, standing over him.

'Sorry to trouble you, Cole, but there's trouble building up and you should oughta nip it in the bud before it flares. A couple of gamblers have taken a big roll off a whiskey-drummer, and now they're making themselves obnoxious to a young woman passenger. I've tried to reason with them but it's no dice. Would you come and cool them off?'

Shand got to his feet and pushed his hat to the back of his head. He was on duty twenty-four hours of the day, and keen on maintaining the smooth running of the line to enhance its reputation of being the safest way to travel through the wilder reaches of the West. He eased his pistol in its low-hung holster and followed O'Toole forward through the swaying coaches. They were still some twenty-odd miles from Longhorn Crossing.

There was tension in the leading coach. Shand entered to find a slim, attractive, dark-haired girl seated between two men. She looked upset by their close attentions, for they were hemming her in on the seat, faces thrust towards her. Both men were smartly dressed in store suits, and each was indelibly stamped with the traits of the professional gambler. Shand had, several times, ejected men of this breed off the company's trains to protect the passengers.

'Are these men bothering you, miss?' Shand enquired.

The girl looked up at him with immeasurable relief dawning in her eyes. She nodded. Both men glanced round. A snarl appeared on the face of the man on her right, revealing large teeth beyond thin lips.

'Get to hell outa here, bozo!' he grated, sliding his right hand under the lapel of his jacket towards an ominous bulge in his left armpit.

Shand palmed his Colt in a blur of speed and crashed the long barrel against the man's flat-crowned Stetson. The man fell back in his seat and took no further interest in the proceedings. His companion eased away from the girl, flicked the fingers of his right hand, and a .41 single-shot derringer slid into his palm on a quick-fire rig attached to his wrist. Shand fired instantly, his bullet taking the gambler in the centre of the chest. The derringer was triggered by a convulsive finger, its owner already dead, and the bullet passed through the roof of the coach.

The girl flinched at the crash of the shots. Gun smoke drifted upwards. Shand grasped the unconscious gambler by his collar and dragged him off the seat. He disarmed the man as a matter of course before turning his attention to the dead man, and removing him roughly. He shook his head and held out a big hand to the girl.

'I'm sorry about the shooting,' he said smoothly. 'Let me escort you to another seat. Are you getting off at Longhorn Crossing?'

She nodded. Her face was ashen, her dark eyes wide, filled with shock. Shand slid a hand under her left elbow and drew her away from the scene. A small, narrow-shouldered man, dressed in a crumpled brown store suit and clutching a big leather sample-case, looked up at Shand from a nearby seat. His face was lined with a network of fine wrinkles.

'Those two gamblers cheated me out of a large sum of money,' he complained.

'I'll get to you in a moment,' Shand said curtly.

He settled the girl in a seat away from the spot she had occupied and returned to the two gamblers. O'Toole was searching the pockets of the dead gambler, and drew a fat leather billfold from inside the bloodstained jacket. The whiskey-drummer craned forward eagerly, holding out a trembling hand.

'They took me for two hundred bucks,' he declared. 'I'm Art Kyle. I didn't want to play. They menaced me into a game, and I could see them cheating but dared not brace them. They would have killed me for sure.'

O'Toole counted out $200 and gave them to the drummer.

'You'll be getting out at Longhorn Crossing, Kyle,' Shand said. 'Go see Ben Trask, the town marshal, and make a statement about what happened here.'

'Sure thing, Mr Shand. I read about you in the El Paso *Gazette* a couple of months ago. There was a picture of you. You're doing a good job for the railroad.'

'Put that in writing and send it to my head office.'

9

Shand grinned. He gave O'Toole a hand to place the dead gambler on the floor between two empty seats. 'Find something to cover him with,' he said. 'I'll take the other into the caboose.'

O'Toole nodded. 'I'm glad you're back on the job, Cole. Hardcases have become a nuisance since they learned you were shot. A passenger was robbed on this run only last week. I've sure noticed the difference while you've been off duty. No one runs the troubleshooting like you.'

'They'll soon get the word I'm back. Watch this one until I come back to him.' Shand went to where the girl was seated and sat down beside her. 'Are you OK?' he asked.

'Yes. Thank you for stepping in. I was really frightened.'

'It's all part of the job, Miss. I'm Cole Shand, chief troubleshooter for the railroad company. Are you visiting folks in Longhorn Crossing?'

'My aunt owns the restaurant there.'

'Abby Swain? I know her well. I always eat at Abby's when I'm in town. She's an old friend. Are you planning on staying around?'

'I'm hoping Abby will suggest it. I lived in St Louis. My mother died a couple of months ago. My father was killed in an accident in Colorado four years ago. He was a mining engineer.' She paused, and then added, 'I'm Barbara Madden.'

'Glad to know you, Miss Madden. Sounds like you've had it rough. And you'll find life in a one-horse town like Longhorn Crossing mighty different from St Louis. Folks out here have a different slant on life. You might find it boring after the big city.'

'Anything for a quiet life,' she responded.

Shand regarded her profile as she watched the desolate scenery flashing by the window. She looked most attractive wearing a long green travelling-dress with a pert pale-green hat perched on long, dark hair. Her brown eyes were showing traces of shock and a frown marred her forehead but did not detract from her beauty. He felt a strand of interest unwind in his mind and tried to suppress it, for he was in the middle of a tough chore and aware that he would need all of his attention focused on it to handle the final play awaiting his return to duty. A pang of emotion filtered through his breast and he crushed it ruthlessly.

'I hope you'll find what you're looking for,' he said. 'I'll see you around, huh? If you'll excuse me, I'll run a check over the train for more undesirables.'

He withdrew quietly and went back to the gamblers. O'Toole was holding a pistol on the uninjured gambler, who had recovered his senses, and Shand took the man with him through the coaches to the caboose at the rear of the train. His thoughts were busy as he considered what might be lying ahead. That last showdown had knocked the resistance out of HTR, but he was not fooled into thinking they had quit. When they had recruited fresh bullies and laid new plans the trouble would resume, and he had to be on his toes if he hoped to quell them again.

The gambler sat motionless in a corner until the train pulled into Longhorn Crossing, which was the end of the line as far as passengers were concerned. The last report he had received told Shand that new track had been laid to thirty-five miles west of the town, and there were 270 miles remaining to Indian Pass, with no other town east of that natural gap in the High Sierras. Shand took the gambler with him when he alighted, and stood watching the dozen passengers alighting and mingling with the few townsfolk who had come to meet the train.

He saw Barbara Madden embrace the matronly figure of Abby Swain. The whiskey-drummer stumbled down the steps of the coach, clutching his sample case to his chest, regained his balance, and scuttled away out of the depot to hurry towards the main street. The half-smile on Shand's lips faded when he saw the chunky figure of Frank Merrick, the district superintendent, appear in the doorway of the depot office.

Merrick was middle-aged, just under six feet in height, his heavy face dark-skinned, his pugnacious jaw covered with black stubble that showed a liberal sprinkling of grey in its midst. His dark eyes glinted with pleasure as he came towards Shand, smiling, hand outstretched in welcome. He had been the chief troubleshooter before Shand, and had groomed the younger man for the job. They were more than colleagues, Merrick having reared Shand from when he was orphaned at ten years old.

'You're a sight for sore eyes, Cole,' Merrick growled. 'It's about time you stopped lazing around in El Paso and came back to the job. How you doing? Is the shoulder better now? Things have been hanging fire while you've been on your back.'

'Have HTR started their play again?' Shand asked quickly.

'Not yet. But the word is that Henry Padlow is busy recruiting more bully-boys to replace the crew you shot to pieces. There's talk that Bo Harmer is gonna run things for HTR now Poggin is in jail, with Henry Padlow bossing Harmer.'

'Harmer's an outlaw.' Shand frowned. 'They won't be able to get away with that. Every lawman in the country will be out after Harmer if he shows his face working for HTR.' He rubbed a hand across his clean-shaven chin. 'I want to talk to you about our future policy, Frank. I know you've turned down my pet idea a couple of times in the past, but after that last showdown we know HTR won't pull any punches, and the sensible thing to do is retaliate. If I took our crew of troubleshooters to HTR's end of track and put them out of business permanent, our troubles would be over, and then some.'

'I've always agreed in principle with that, Cole.' Merrick shook his head. 'While I was doing your job I always believed in fighting fire with fire. But I've had strict orders from higher up – from TC Jeffery, the chief executive, no less. He doesn't want that kind of trouble on his plate any more. Times are changing back East faster than they are around here. It's OK for HTR to employ such tactics but not us. Violence is bad for business. We're gonna have to do it the hard way now, so forget retaliation. Are you fit to take over your job?'

'I'd still be in El Paso if I wasn't fit. Have you got a

length of rope, Frank?'

'Rope? Whaddya want with a piece of rope?'

'So you can tie my hands behind my back before I restart the job.' Shand grinned and slapped Merrick's thick shoulder. 'What's doing with Poggin? Has he been in court yet? I hope you've added murder in the first degree to his charges. I saw him shoot Jim Bowen in the back.'

'Yeah. We're throwing the book at him. He's wanted for other murders, anyway, and he'll sure swing for what he's done. His trial starts in a week or so.'

'Is he still in the calaboose here?'

'Yeah. His trial is being held in town, and they're gonna make a big thing of it. I'll be glad when it's all over, Cole, and no mistake. Everything seems to be suspended until Poggin has been dealt with. I had to put a new man in your job while you've been laid up.'

'Bill Clayton? He's the best there is. He's been my deputy for more than a year now, and he's been waiting to step into my boots. You couldn't find a better man if you needed to replace me.'

Merrick shook his head. 'I put Clayton in charge but head office sent me a new man, Jack Sawtell, a detective from back East. TC Jeffery wants to get away from the image of the old-style troubleshooter.' Disgust sounded in Merrick's tone. 'Can you believe that? Instead of shooting the hell out of the opposition, which we both know is the only way to handle the job, they want a top-class detective to go out, gather proof of wrong-doing, then arrest the guilty men like they do in New York.'

'So am I out of a job? Shand demanded.

'Hell no! Sawtell has been poking around at end of track for about a month, and so far he's come up with nothing. I didn't tell him he's wasting his time, but he's reaching that conclusion himself now, I shouldn't wonder. I reckon he'll report that there's nothing he can do and head back to where he came from. When HTR hits us again, you'll be right back in business.'

Shand considered for a moment, thinking over the situation. Then he told Merrick about the two gamblers on the train.

'Jeez! Did you have to kill one of them?' Merrick demanded. 'You're not back on duty officially yet, and now there's another dead man.' He turned to the silent gambler standing submissively by Shand's side. 'Go on, get outa here before I'm tempted to kill you,' he rapped. 'Don't let me see your face on our trains after this.'

The gambler nodded, stammered his thanks, and hurried off into the town.

'I sure wish there was an easier way of doing my job,' Shand said softly. 'Why don't you get the top brass up to end of track and let them see for themselves how it works for us? I'm getting a mite tired of setting myself up as a target. I've taken four slugs in my five years as chief troubleshooter, and let me tell you what I'm thinking these days, Frank – the job ain't worth a light! I must be touched in the head to do it.'

'You got my sympathy, Cole.' Merrick turned away. 'There's a work train going to end of track in the

15

morning. I reckon you'll wanta be on it. Check around and stay out of trouble for a few days. Work your way back into the routine quietly, and I'll try and keep those bozos in head office off your neck.'

Merrick went back into his office. Shand started to follow but turned as the conductor came up to him, carrying Shand's carpetbag.

'Are you staying, Cole?' he asked.

'Have you heard something that Frank hasn't told me?' Shand countered, grinning harshly. 'I've just heard about the new non-violence rule, and I don't like it.'

'Nope. But I've heard the talk, like everybody else. I think the same as Frank does, you know that. They're gonna need men like you for a long time to come, and take it from me, Cole, we ain't seen the worst of it yet. The nearer we move to Indian Pass, the more desperate HTR are gonna get.'

'That's obvious to me.' Shand narrowed his eyes as he watched the passengers departing from the depot. 'But I don't have to worry about the railroad's reputation. All I have to do is shoot any trouble that comes up, and get shot in my turn. It's the helluva note when the big brass won't face up to facts. If we don't hit HTR hard then we'll lose this fight, and you know who they'll blame.'

'You, huh? There ain't no justice in this world, Cole.' O'Toole spoke sadly.

Shand took his bag and left the depot. He paused outside to look around the main street of Longhorn Crossing. Nothing seemed to have changed since his departure more than two months before, and his mind flicked up pictures of the big showdown that had temporarily busted HTR's ability to cause trouble. He moved on, heading for the law office, wanting to confront Nat Poggin, for he had some unfinished business with the imprisoned badman.

Ben Trask, the town marshal, was standing in the doorway of the law office. He was getting too old for his job, and knew it, but kept the knowledge to himself. He was in his middle fifties. His reflexes were slowing and he no longer had the vitality with which he had pursued law-dealing in his younger days. If the railroad had not come through town on its way to Indian Pass he would not have been caught up in the lawlessness that attended the event and might have retired before now, but he felt obliged to stay until railroad business had been settled. He had to steel himself to get up each morning and force himself to face the day with equanimity. He had always trusted his instincts, and for some time now they had been warning him to quit.

Shand looked critically at Trask, noting the man's altered looks, and could see that the recent troubles had taken their toll of the town marshal. Trask looked ten years older than the last time Shand had seen him. His eyes held a haunted expression and his appearance was ragged at the edges. He seemed to be holding himself together with some desperation.

'Howdy, Cole. Good to see you back.' A reluctant smile flickered across Trask's thin lips. 'You look a lot better than the last time I saw you. Are you back on the job now?'

'Sure, Ben, and raring to go. I'll be heading out to

17

end of track in the morning. How you making out with Poggin behind bars?'

'He don't bother me none. He'll be gone in a couple of weeks. They'll hang him for sure. It's an open-and-shut case. Your evidence alone will set him swinging by the neck. I'm glad you're back, Cole. I need to talk to you. I got a bad feeling that someone will make a try to bust Poggin out of here. HTR want him back because he played up hell with your railroad until you nailed him. I've asked for more deputies, but the town says they can't afford them. I'm practically on my own here, and couldn't do much if a hard bunch rode in to spring Poggin loose.'

Shand frowned. 'Have you talked to Frank about this?' he asked. 'I reckon Poggin is railroad business.'

'Yeah. So does Frank, but he says his hands are tied. What happens in law is not in his book. He said I've only got to yell and he'll come running, but if anything happens it'll be all over before anyone in town learns about it.'

'I'll detail a couple of men to keep an eye on the jail until Poggin's trial is over.' Shand frowned. 'I can't believe Frank hasn't taken steps. If Poggin gets away we'll be right back where we were before that last showdown.'

'Don't put yourself in wrong with your people,' Trask said quickly.

'Ben, while I'm running this business I'll do as I see fit. If my way of handling trouble doesn't suit those bozos at head office then they can find someone else to do their dirty work. I'd like to see Poggin now. I've been waiting to have a talk with him.'

'Sure. Come on in.' Trask grinned. 'Poggin will be right pleased to see you.'

Shand followed the marshal into the office and dropped his bag into a corner. Trask picked up the cell keys from his desk and crossed to the door leading into the big back room where the cells were. Shand fought down his tension as he followed. The last time he'd seen Poggin the showdown had been raging, and he'd had many sleepless nights since, trying to come to terms with the violence that had wiped out HTR's bid for supremacy and killed several of his colleagues. He had a sneaking feeling that the shoot-out had left its indelible mark on him, and hoped it would not affect him the next time he went into action.

TWO

Nat Poggin was tall, broad-shouldered and powerful. He was lying on his back on the bunk in a corner cell, his hands behind his head; his hard face set as if it had been carved from stone. His black hair was a tangled mass that hung over his forehead and his dark eyes glared balefully at Shand as the troubleshooter paused before the door of the cell. Marshal Trask stood in the background, his unblinking gaze intent upon his notorious prisoner.

'So you ain't dead!' Poggin spoke in a deep voice that seemed to start in his boots. 'I'm disappointed, Shand. I was hopin' I'd seen the last of you. But you ain't gonna live to see me hang. The word is out that you'll collect a slug soon as you're back. Do you think HTR have changed their minds about getting to Indian Pass before you? No chance! They'll be back with a bigger and better crew, and you'll be the first on their list.'

'If you've got nothing better to say then keep your lip buttoned.' Shand spoke through his teeth. He had a picture in his mind of Jim Bowen dropping with a bullet in his back – fired by Poggin. 'You better start worrying about your future. Your trial starts soon, and they ain't gonna waste any time. I'll be watching when they swing you into hell.'

'You'll be there waiting to welcome me if that day comes.' Poggin grinned and pushed himself up off the bunk. He came towards the door of the cell but paused just out of arm's length. His grey shirt was unbuttoned, revealing a swath of bandages around his barrel-like chest. 'You had your chance but you couldn't kill me. You put two bullets in me and missed the vital spot. I nicked you with a slug but I was going down then, and the next time I draw a bead on you I won't make any mistake. I'll plug you dead centre.'

'You're not as tough as you think.' Shand smiled. 'When you begin to feel the rope choking off your air you'll change your tune, and I'll be waiting to hear you wailing on your way out. It won't do you any good to start calling for mercy after you're sentenced. Just remember that I gave you a chance to co-operate, but you turned me down. So be it!'

'If you want me to co-operate then open this door and put a gun in my hand.' Poggin grinned.

'You wouldn't want to face me,' Shand replied, 'unless my back was to you.' He turned away from the door. 'I can see it's a waste of time talking to you. See you in court, Poggin.'

'Not if I have anything to do with it,' Poggin replied.

Shand went back into the front office. Trask locked the heavy door separating the office from the cell block. His face was grim as he walked to his desk.

'I'll be glad when this is done,' he said. 'Poggin gets to me.'

'I was hoping a couple of months behind bars would have loosened his tongue, but he'll never talk. Has anyone been in to see him?'

'Only Merrick when he brought in that detective from back East. I didn't cotton to him, the way he asked fool questions. His way of working in New York ain't good around here.'

'I'll have a couple of my men covering you until the trial is over, Ben.' Shand was determined there would be no mistakes made around Poggin. 'We don't want Poggin escaping now we've got him in a hole.'

'Will Merrick go along with that? I mentioned it to him and he didn't wanta know. He said something about a change of policy at head office. They think there's been too much violence. Instead of settling the trouble here with hot lead, they plan to do it from an office back East – SWRR and HTR sitting around a table and talking money, which is what it is all about when you get down to brass tacks.'

Shand smiled and walked to the door. He paused and looked back at Trask, whose gaunt face was showing worry.

'They can talk all they want, but there's only one way to settle this trouble and that's by shooting the hell out of it. Too many good men have been killed trying to do their duty for anything else to work.'

'That's what I'm afraid of.' Trask nodded. 'Watch your step, Cole. Poggin ain't the kind to make idle threats. He talks as if he knows something we don't.

You're the one man who can hold this business in check, and if HTR can get you SWRR will be finished.'

'It's a pity TC Jeffery can't see it that way. I'll pick up my bag later, Ben.'

Shand departed and stood on the street looking around at the unlovely town, his eyes narrowed and his thoughts racing. On an impulse he walked back to the railroad depot and entered Frank Merrick's office. Merrick was seated at his desk, wading through a stack of paperwork. He shook his head and sighed heavily when he looked up.

'If you've got nothing to do until that supply train arrives tomorrow morning then you can pull up a chair and gimme a hand with this lot,' he said harshly. 'I can remember the day when there was damn-all paperwork. Now all I seem to do is sift through a mountain of the stuff.'

'I'm not happy that Ben Trask has got no support at the jail,' Shand cut in. 'He said he spoke to you about having a couple of special deputies. We lost some good men nailing Poggin, and there he sits in jail with just a single lawman guarding him. I'm surprised he hasn't been busted out before now.'

'Yeah. I guess you're right.' Merrick shook his head. 'I got so damn much on my plate these days. Set a couple of men to guarding the jail until the trial is over.'

'What men have I got and where will I find them?' Shand demanded.

'You'll have to find them. I set them to riding the track watching for trouble, checking trestles and so on. They report in regularly. There was nothing else I could do while you were away, and it's been quiet. No trouble from HTR since the big showdown.'

'Frank, you know patrolling the track ain't the way to fight HTR. They could hit us in a hundred places without being seen, and get away with it. We couldn't guard the line properly even if we had an army in our pay. We have to change our tactics or lose out. I've had time to think about it while I've been laid up, and I can see what went before.'

'Did you come up with a way to beat HTR?' Merrick studied Shand's intense expression, noting the strain showing there; unmistakable signs of shock and weakness. 'You don't look like you're fit yet to return to duty,' he said softly. 'Mebbe you should take another week or so and give yourself time to recollect yourself.'

'I'm OK,' Shand said tightly. 'It won't hurt me to look around and tighten our defences where I see problems. What we really need are more men.'

'Recruits are turning up all the time – hardcases and gunhands all looking for a pay-off. I've set some of them on, but you'll need to check them out. There's a bunch of them living rough around town. They've made the saloon their headquarters, and as soon as they get the word that you're back they'll be after you like a bunch of redskins, all clamouring for a job.'

'OK.' Shand nodded. 'I'll start recruiting. Have you got anyone watching HTR? We need to know what they're up to.'

'Joe Tolliver was handling that chore, and he was

found dead last week, shot in the back. Knowing you were on the point of returning, I didn't set anyone else on that particular chore.'

'Passing the buck again, huh?' Shand grinned tightly. 'I heard Joe was killed. I'd better get to work. I'll let you have a list of new men, if I set anyone on. See you later, Frank.'

Merrick nodded and returned to his paperwork. Shand left the office and went along the street to the Red Steer saloon. A voice hailed him as he reached the batwings, and he turned to see Bill Clayton coming across the street.

'Hey, Cole, it's good to see you back! How you doing?' Clayton greeted.

'Howdy, Bill. Glad to be back. Come and have a drink and tell me what's been going on since I dropped out.'

'You won't like any of it.' Clayton was tall and thin, in his middle twenties, with brown eyes and black hair. He was dressed in a blue store suit and shoes, and wore a cartridge-belt around his slim waist, its holster containing a Remington .44. The brim of a grey Stetson was pulled low over his sharp gaze. He was one of the few men Shand knew he could trust, and they had been friends for a long time, their relationship tested and proved many times in the execution of the arduous duty they performed for the railroad.

'I've been getting some of the story from Frank and it ain't good. The brass back East are getting nervous about the way we're shooting trouble. The law is strong back there, and they don't seem to grasp the degree of trouble we have to face. But all they're really interested in is profit, and they won't do anything except complain so long as the coffers continue to fill. But I'm running this job, and I'll do it my way until they decide to get rid of me.'

'That's the way it goes.' Clayton pushed open the batwings and led the way into the saloon. 'I've got half a dozen men lined up for work, and I expect they're in here, waiting for you to look them over. The trouble has attracted all kinds, Cole, but you can tell at a glance which ones are unsuitable. I've been watching for bad guys who have been set on us by HTR. They ain't so easy to spot, but one man has turned up who I think was running with HTR before the showdown. I reckon he's been sent here to work undercover against us.'

'Where is he?' Shand looked around the big saloon room. There were at least twenty men present, some drinking at the bar and others playing cards at the sprinkling of gaming-tables occupying the centre space.

Clayton moved to the near end of the bar and signalled to the tender.

'He's at that corner table – tall man with the red shirt. Chuck Henry. He told me he'd come down from Kansas, but I've got a feeling I saw him in El Paso about three months ago in the bunch Nat Poggin was bossing. He showed up here last week asking for a start and I told him to stick around until you got back. He has a sidekick with him, who I don't see here right now; man named Elmer Pierce. They both seem to have money to spend, not like the other hardcases looking for work. I reckon they're being paid by HTR.'

'I saw Poggin this morning and he reckons I'll be dead before he comes to trial,' Shand mused. 'Henry and Pierce might be the men they've sent in to nail me, or bust Poggin out of jail. I want a couple of good men to stand by the jail as special deputies until the trial takes place. Who have we got we can trust, Bill?'

'Pat Eke is a good man; him and his sidekick Tom Baldwin. Eke has been complaining about the lack of action. I told him things would liven up when you came back.'

'Warn them to stand by the jail. They'll take orders from Trask. Whatever happens, Poggin must not escape. Tell them to kill him if there's any trouble and it looks like he might get away.'

The tender came to them and Shand asked for two beers.

'Pat and Tom are both out of town at the moment,' Clayton said, 'riding the rails from here to end of track. I'm expecting them back later today.'

'And we need someone to take over Tolliver's job of watching HTR. How did they get wise to him? Is someone in our crew drawing pay from them? I heard that Bo Harmer is running the show for HTR now Poggin is out of circulation. I met him once, before all the trouble started, and I figured then that he was a clever man – devious, and then some. Maybe we'll have to send someone to put him out of action.'

'Merrick wouldn't stand for downright murder. Since that last showdown he's been yelling about

27

cutting out the violence, but he knows we ain't calling the tune. HTR is the one using dirty tricks, and so far all we've done is fight them off.'

'That's why I want to change the pattern some.' Shand's eyes narrowed as he looked around the big saloon room. 'We've got to start calling the shots, Bill.' He picked up one of the two glasses of foaming beer sent along the bar by the tender, took a long pull at the contents, and then wiped his mouth with the back of his right hand. 'We'll adapt the orders Frank gives us so we have the edge all the time. Don't let this go any further, but I don't aim to fight with one hand tied behind my back.'

'It's about time we got wise to the situation,' Clayton agreed. 'We're the ones doing the fighting, and it's a real war out there, so let's do it right, huh?'

'You're damn right.' Shand finished his beer. 'OK. So let's get to work. Hey, Mack,' he called to the tender. 'Can I use a back room to talk to some of these men? I need to recruit a new crew.'

'Sure thing, Cole.' Mack Harper mopped his sweating brow. 'It's about time you got down to cases. These guys are running me off my feet.'

Shand walked to the rear of the saloon and Clayton accompanied him.

'Send them in one at a time, Bill,' Shand said.

'It'll be my pleasure. I don't like the feeling of being undermanned. HTR could give us our come-uppance now, if they did but know the facts.'

'They've missed their chance, and we'll have to try and take advantage of that lapse. Let's get this over with as soon as we can. I don't have much interest in work at the moment.'

Clayton grinned and Shand went into the back room of the saloon. He sat down at a table to await the first of the would-be troubleshooters. He saw nine men in all and set on six of them, including Chuck Henry and EImer Pierce. He had his doubts about both men when he saw them, and could well believe that they were working undercover for HTR. Henry was big and shifty-eyed, and there was an indefinable trait in his manner that rubbed Shand up the wrong way. Pierce seemed OK, but indicated that he always worked with Henry and they should be considered as a pair. Shand took them on in order to keep an eye on them, and left Clayton to organize the recruits into a working group.

He went back to the bar and tried to relax with another beer. One of the men he had turned down came to his side and called for a drink.

'I got no hard feelings about not getting a job with you, Shand,' the man said. 'I admire what you're doing, and everyone knows how HTR are hitting you below the belt. I reckon you should know that I heard Chuck Henry and his sidekick talking about how they're gonna put one over on you. From what they said, my guess is that they're drawing pay from HTR, so you better watch that pair.'

'What's your name?' Shand looked the young man.

'Pete Howlett.'

Shand nodded, taking a closer look at Howlett, who had almost passed a first scrutiny for a job. The man was clean and looked presentable.

'Yeah. I turned you down because you've had no experience on the railroad and I need men who are handy with a gun. So what else did you hear?'

'There are four men in town who reckon to bust open the jail and turn Nat Poggin loose.'

'Have you seen those men?'

'Sure. They've been hanging around with Chuck Henry.'

'Do you still want a job with SWRR?'

'I'd like nothing better, and I will use a gun if I have to.'

'OK. You're on. Where are those four now?'

'You've taken on two of them; Henry and Pierce. The other two are over there at that corner table. Joe Doyle is wearing a blue shirt and black hat and Bat Hayman is the man opposite him in the red shirt.'

'Watch Doyle and Hayman. Learn what you can about their plans. Leave Henry and Pierce to me. I'll set up a welcome for them when they go to the jail for Poggin.'

'Sure thing.' Howlett moved away immediately.

Shand gazed after him with speculative gaze before finishing his beer. He left the saloon. The street was quiet. He looked around and saw Abby Swain standing at the door to her restaurant with her niece Barbara Madden. The two women were talking animatedly. Shand walked in their direction, his gaze on the girl's face. She was attractive, and he liked the look of her. Not many women appealed to him because he did not permit them to gain his interest, but this girl had penetrated his defences with ease and he approached her with anticipation surging through him.

'Cole!' Abby Swain broke off her conversation and looked up at him as Shand reached her. She smiled expansively, her fleshy face beaming as she regarded him. She was short and amply built, her blue eyes filled with a glint that spoke of an indomitable spirit. She was probably forty years old, and the rigours of the climate showed in her face. 'Barbara told me about that shooting on the train. It's a good thing you're back now. Have you recovered from your wound?'

'Yes thanks, Abby. I'm over the worst of it. I'm glad I was on hand when those gamblers acted up. I guess they hadn't heard I was back.'

'It was frightening,' Barbara said in a low, intense tone. 'They didn't act like any men I ever knew. I feared they would harm me, and when you confronted them they turned on you like a pair of wild animals.'

'It was all part of my job,' Shand said. 'I've been away for two months and some men took advantage of the fact. Now I'm back I hope to keep the railroad clear of their kind.'

'You've still got a lot of trouble on your plate, Cole, according to what I'm hearing.' Abby's pleasant face was twisted into a mask of concern. 'Frank Merrick was telling me about the new policy his bosses have adopted. You can't use violence any more.'

'That will never work.' Shand shook his head impatiently. 'The bosses can come out here and show us how to operate their new policy, and we'll bury them after their first attempt. I won't stand for any curbs. If they try that then they can find another man to handle it. If I put my life on the line again it will be on my terms. I don't plan to have my hands tied by any Easterner.'

'That's the way to talk,' Abby approved. 'Come in for a meal. We were about to eat. Barbara is gonna stay with me, and I hope to get her involved in my business. I've told her she could do worse than look to you for guidance around here.'

'I'm afraid I'm gonna be too busy to spare time for anything but my job.' Shand shook his head. 'And from the way it looks, life will be plumb unhealthy around me. I wouldn't advise anyone, man or woman, to get too close. I've already got reports of trouble brewing and I haven't been back an hour. Life ain't gonna get easier, that's a fact.'

He saw Barbara suppress a shudder at his words as he escorted both women into the restaurant, and he joined them in a private room to enjoy a noonday meal. He tried to relax in their company but thoughts of his grim business were prodding him like a broken spur. He could not enjoy the pleasant diversion of their company and escaped at the earliest possible moment, complimenting Abby on her usual high standard of cuisine, and promising to visit again.

Outside, he braced himself to return to duty, his keen blue eyes taking details of the street. He was feeling far from ready to start working. His mind was protesting against the strictures being placed upon him, and he was hoping that trouble was still far off. His teeth clicked together when he saw Ben Trask standing in the doorway of the law office, waving a hand to attract his attention. He suppressed a sigh and went along the sidewalk, his keen gaze taking in his surroundings. He was coiled as tight as a spring inside, and tension filled his big figure as the fingers of his right hand brushed the black butt of his holstered pistol.

'Cole, there are a couple of men skulking in the alley across the street,' Trask said tightly as soon as Shand was within earshot. 'I spotted them as you went into Abby's place. It looks like they're on the prod.'

Shand turned and placed his back against the front wall of the law office, his gaze sweeping the shadowed side of the street. He saw movement in an alley opposite and his pistol came readily into his hand. Two men stepped out of the alley at that precise moment, and one was holding a drawn six-gun. Shand dropped to one knee as a shot crashed and a puff of smoke plumed towards him. He heard the crackle of a .45 slug as it passed his left ear and thudded into the front wall of the law office. His uneasiness fled then and he was relieved that the action had started.

THREE

Shand's pistol hammered as he sent two quick shots across the street. He was dimly aware that bullets were smacking into the wall behind him. He squinted as gun smoke flared, and was gratified to see one of the men pitching into the dust. Acrid smoke stung his nostrils. He fired again, hardly seeming to aim, and his slug hit the second man in the same instant that Ben Trask triggered his gun. Two bullets hit the assailant in the chest, sending him twisting to the ground. It was a familiar scene to Shand's eyes, and he moistened his lips in distaste.

He remained motionless, his pistol upraised while he looked around for further trouble. Echoes were fading slowly. He got to his feet. The few townsfolk on the street were frozen in shock at the violent disturbance. Shand went to Trask's side. The town marshal's face was set in a blank mask, but he grinned tensely when he met Shand's steady gaze.

'I'd been watching them for some time,' Trask said. 'I had a feeling they were after you. I saw you go into the restaurant with Abby and her niece, and those two skulked around over there until you

34

showed again. Let's take a look at them.'

'Sure.' Shand holstered his gun with a slick movement. 'I've got a couple of men to act as your special
deputies; Pat Eke and Tom Baldwin. You can have
them until after Poggin's trial. I've heard there are
four men in town talking about busting Poggin out,
but I don't believe these are two of them. It looks like
HTR are going whole hog to knock us out of business.'

'It's been quiet while you were away,' Trask mused.
'They've been waiting for you to come back, Cole.'

'That's the way it goes.' Shand started across the
street, which was now alive with movement. Several
townsmen were converging on the law office. Bill
Clayton was coming along the sidewalk, a pistol in his
hand, and Frank Merrick was in view at the depot,
holding a shotgun and watching closely.

The two dead men were strangers to Shand. He
gazed down at them with no hint of concern in his
features, but he felt cold inside.

'I've never seen either of them before,' Trask
commented.

'I have,' Clayton said, coming up. 'Looks like the
game is starting sooner than we expected, Cole. It's
been quiet around here while you've been away. That
should tell you something, huh?'

Shand saw Abby Swain and her niece standing in
front of the restaurant, watching intently, and experienced a strand of emotion in his breast. He was
becoming certain that the showdown two months
before had affected him adversely and its effects were
coming to the surface with the recommencement of

violence. He wondered if he had lost his nerve, but he felt no sense of fear. The job had always been one with the single inflexible rule of 'kill or be killed', and he had never experienced one sleepless night over any of the men he had shot. He saw Frank Merrick coming along the street and turned to meet him.

'Get these two off the street, Bill,' he said over his shoulder. 'Try to identify them, huh?'

Merrick's face was set in grave lines. The butt of his shotgun was tucked under his right armpit. He halted an arm's length from Shand and stood shaking his head slowly.

'I don't know how anyone can believe that we can resolve our problems without gun-play,' he observed.

'Don't worry about it.' Shand forced a grin. 'We both know what has to be done, and this trouble is a long way from being finished. Apart from this trouble, I've heard there are four men in town right now who are planning to bust Poggin out of jail.'

'So why the hell are you standing here talking about it? Shouldn't you be doing something about them?'

'I have already. I'll be warned when they start to make their move, and a quick swoop will nail them. But let's get the rules right before I go any further, Frank. Do I carry on as before or has the policy been changed?'

'Nothing has changed as far as I'm concerned,' Merrick said sharply. 'Go about your business the only way it can be done, and I'll keep the fools at head office off your neck. Nail 'em all, Cole. Give 'em hell.'

Shand nodded and turned away, drawing his pistol to reload the spent chambers. He went back to where Clayton and Trask were standing over the dead men, and now half a dozen townsmen were gathering around in a little knot, all gazing stolidly at the bloodstained figures.

'Bill, come with me,' Shand said, and motioned for Trask to accompany them as they walked along the street towards the saloon. 'I'm after Chuck Henry and Pierce. I was gonna wait for them to tip their hand but we'll play it safe and pick them up now. There are two others who might be HTR men – Doyle and Hayman. I've got Pete Howlett watching them, so we'll make a start with Henry and his side-kick.'

'They'll be passing their time in the saloon,' Clayton said. 'I told them to be at the depot tomorrow morning ready to pull out on the work train.'

'They're not going to end of track. We're taking them out now.'

Clayton grinned and dropped his right hand to the butt of his Remington. They went on, and Shand glanced at Trask as they reached the law office. The marshal's face was grim, but he grinned when he met Shand's gaze.

'We going after Henry and Pierce, and will need you along to make it legal, Ben,' Shand said.

'Sure. Have you got proof against them?' Trask lengthened his stride to get abreast of Shand. 'I guess that's a silly question, huh?'

'We got them dead to rights,' Shand replied.

They reached the saloon and entered. Clayton

thrust open the batwings and their boots thudded on the pine boards inside. Heads turned at their entrance. Shand's keen gaze swept over the men present and he spotted Chuck Henry and Elmer Pierce sitting at a corner table. Pete Howlett was at the same table, with Doyle and Hayman standing behind him. Shand's eyes narrowed. He saw that Howlett's holster was empty, and tensed his right hand at his side, his fingers brushing the butt of his gun.

'Bill, watch Doyle and Hayman,' Shand said. 'Ben, play it as it comes.'

All noise in the saloon had ceased at their appearance, Shand noticed, as they walked towards the corner table. He halted six feet from the seated group, who were motionless, gazing up with sudden indecision showing on their faces, as if Shand's arrival had surprised them in some nefarious activity. Chuck Henry's mouth opened as if he were about to speak, and then clamped shut and his eyes changed expression.

'Don't do anything with your hands,' Shand rapped. 'We're taking you and your pards in, Henry.'

Chuck Henry surged to his feet, overturning the table with his powerful body. Pete Howlett dived sideways as the table went over. Shand palmed his gun and it was cocked and ready for action before Henry could draw his pistol. Shand fired, aiming for Henry's right shoulder. Henry cleared leather, but a .45 slug smashed through flesh and bone in his upper arm and his weapon fell from his hand. Action spread like wildfire.

The saloon rocked to heavy detonations. Doyle and Hayman were swinging around to face Shand, both making a play for their holstered guns, and Clayton triggered his pistol rapidly. Pierce was at a disadvantage with the table toppling over on him and threw himself to one side, trying to get at his holstered gun, but the table balked him, and by the time he rolled clear he found himself staring into the black muzzle of Shand's pistol.

Doyle hit the floor with blood pouring out of a wound in his throat. Hayman threw down his gun and raised his hands. Pete Howlett regained his feet, face pale, eyes filled with shock. Henry was lying on the floor on his face, unmoving, and blood was staining his shirt around his shoulder and upper arm. Gun echoes faded slowly. Shand drew a deep breath of smoke-filled air, his heart thudding powerfully.

'What happened to you, Howlett?' Shand asked. 'You were sitting with these buzzards with no gun in your holster.'

'Doyle and Hayman got the drop on me,' Howlett said. 'They brought me in here to face Henry, who's running things for HTR. When you showed up he was giving them orders to take me out of town and kill me.'

Trask was collecting the guns of the HTR men. The saloon was slowly coming back to life. Shand looked around, then detailed a townsman to fetch the doctor. Hayman and Pierce were standing with their hands raised, their expressions bleak. Trask searched them for hidden weapons, and relieved Hayman of a pistol that was stuck in the back of his belt against his spine.

'That's my gun,' Howlett said, taking it from the town marshal's hand.

Shand bent over Chuck Henry. The man was barely conscious, and groaned when Shand turned him over. His right shoulder was shattered, leaking blood profusely, and he lapsed into unconsciousness, breathing heavily.

Doc Gilroy came bustling into the saloon, carrying a leather medical bag in his right hand. He was tall, and thin like a beanpole, touching sixty, and wore a black store suit that gave him an austere appearance. He wore no hat and his shock of thinning grey hair allowed his skull to show through.

'I was about to sit down to a meal, Cole' he protested. 'I wish you would time your operations better than this. And look where you've shot this man. Can't you hit your victims any place else? It's a helluva job, patching up a busted shoulder; a two-hour job at least.'

'Sorry, Doc.' Shand grimaced. 'I don't pick the time and place, you know, and I always aim for the right shoulder if the man is right-handed, where most of the wounds are not fatal. I need to ask questions, and dead men tell no tales.'

The doctor dropped to one knee beside Chuck Henry and examined the man's shoulder. He arose almost immediately and looked around the saloon, detailing four men to carry Henry along to his office. He checked Doyle, who was dead, and moved off towards the batwings, followed by the four men carrying Henry.

Trask motioned for Hayman and Pierce to move out. Shand told Howlett to go with the doctor and stay with Henry.

'I'll be along later, Pete,' he said. 'Henry won't feel like making a run for it, but I want him watched.'

Howlett nodded and departed. Shand glanced at Clayton.

'Get Joe Ivey to take care of the body, Bill, and then come along to the law office.'

Clayton nodded and Shand followed Trask and the two prisoners out of the saloon. A crowd of townsfolk were standing outside the batwings and they gazed with interest at the prisoners. Part of the crowd followed them to the law office. Hayman and Pierce were taken into the office and Trask escorted Hayman into the cells. Shand began to question Pierce, and soon realized that the man would not co-operate. He wasted no time, warning Pierce that he was facing a charge of attempted murder, which could be dropped if he confessed to his part in HTR's lawless attempts to block SWRR's progress.

Pierce remained silent. Trask emerged from the cells and then took Pierce inside the cell block, locking him in a cell before returning with Hayman, who was looking apprehensive.

'You should look worried, Hayman,' Shand said. 'You're in bad trouble, and no one is gonna help you out of it, except me, maybe. I'll do a deal with you. Tell me what you were planning and who gave the orders, and I'll let you go.'

'I don't know anything about what's going on,'

41

Hayman replied. 'I came into town to get a job with SWRR.'

'Pete Howlett tells a different story,' Shand persisted. 'You and Doyle disarmed him and took him to Chuck Henry. Howlett said Henry told you and Doyle to take him out of town and kill him. If that evidence gets to court against you then you'll spend the rest of your life behind bars. Think about it. I'll come back shortly to talk to you some more, and I hope you'll have worked out your best course of action. You've got to think of yourself in this. HTR won't help you. Play it smart and you could walk away. Put him back in a cell, Ben. I haven't got time to waste.'

Trask nodded and Hayman went back into a cell. Shand followed and stood at the bars of Nat Poggin's cell.

'You were expecting to be sprung out of here today, Poggin,' he remarked, 'and I'm real sorry to disappoint you. I guess we're always gonna beat your crew, and the sooner you get wise to that the better.'

'Get the hell outa here and let me sleep,' Poggin snarled. 'You talk too much, Shand. Gimme a gun with just one shell in it and I'll make you sing a different tune.'

'I'd like nothing better than to take you on, you polecat, but the law needs you, and I'm gonna be behind you every step of the way.' Shand grinned. 'I'll be standing close by when you swing into hell.'

He left the jail and went along the street to the doctor's house. Pete Howlett was sitting on a chair in the office where Doc Gilroy was operating on Chuck

42

Henry. Shand bent over the supine Henry, who was unconscious, and looked at the wound in which Gilroy was probing.

'A forty-five slug sure makes a big hole, huh?' he observed. 'Is it gonna be a long job, Doc?'

'Too damn long! It'll be dark before I sit down to my meal. Why didn't you kill him? It would have saved me a lot of trouble, and you'll probably hang him after all. Can't you shoot straight, Cole? A bullet dead centre would have finished him off neatly.'

'I need him alive to talk about his job,' Shand replied. 'We've got a big battle coming up against HTR. It won't go away, and it'll be a whole lot worse than anything we've seen before. My hands are being tied by the bosses back East, and I'll probably be fired from my job before it's over. And you think you've got problems, Doc!'

'I've heard the talk that's going around.' Gilroy's hands were busy on Henry's shoulder. He straightened, and withdrew a misshapen slug from the gory wound. 'Do you want this back?' he demanded.

'No thanks. I got plenty more where that came from. How soon will Henry be able to talk?'

'I'll keep him sedated. He won't come round before sundown. Drop by in about four hours. If he opens his eyes before then I'll put him under again. Why don't you leave him until tomorrow morning? It'll give him time to collect his thoughts, and he might be ready to talk by then. One thing is for sure – he ain't going anywhere with a wound like this.'

'I know. I collected one just like it a couple of months ago.' Shand turned to leave, but paused beside Howlett. 'Stay here until someone comes to spell you,' he told Howlett. 'Don't let Henry out of your sight.'

'Sure thing.' Howlett nodded.

Shand sighed in relief as he left the doctor's house. He looked around the street. The town was back to normal now. The crowd had dispersed. He walked towards the depot, wanting to talk some more with Frank Merrick, but he was impatient to leave in the morning on the work train for the construction camp at the end of track. He needed to get back into the full flow of the job, which meant fighting all opposition to SWRR's progress.

He suddenly realized that Bill Clayton had not reported back to the law office after seeing the undertaker. He went along to the saloon to peer in over the batwings. The saloon was practically empty now, and he called to the tender, enquiring after Clayton.

'He left about five minutes ago,' Mack Harper replied, 'and looked like he was in a hurry.'

'Any idea where he was going?'

'Nope.' Harper shook his head. 'He didn't say.'

Shand went on to the law office. Trask was seated at his desk, writing a report. The marshal looked up, and then put down his pen.

'Something wrong?' he queried. 'You look like a hungry man who's got something cooking on a slow fire.'

'Bill Clayton should have come here after seeing Joe Ivey about Doyle. Have you seen him, Ben?'

'No. He ain't been around.'

'He left the saloon in a hurry about five minutes ago.' Shand made to depart quickly, but paused in the doorway. 'Have you heard any shooting?' he asked.

'Not a sound. Do you think he's found trouble?' Trask got to his feet and came around the desk. 'I'll go with you to find him,' he said, taking a shotgun from a gunrack. 'There's never a dull moment when you're around, Cole,' he mused.

They walked along the street side by side. Shand was checking the interior of the general store when two quick shots hammered and echoed across the town. Trask set off at a run along the sidewalk.

'That sounded like it came from the livery stable,' Trask shouted over his shoulder.

Shand started running. He passed Trask, drawing his gun as he did so. He saw a rider suddenly emerge from the stable, pause to look around the street, and then jerk a rifle from his saddle scabbard. Shand shouted a warning to Trask and began to weave as the rider lifted the rifle to his shoulder. He raised his pistol and fired a shot at the man, more in the hope of throwing him off his aim than hitting him. The rider fired three shots, two of which whined perilously close to Shand's head, then set off at a gallop out of town. Shand narrowed his eyes; he could not identify the rider, but he noted the horse and reckoned he would know it if he saw it again. He was breathless when he reached the stable, and he halted in the doorway, his gaze picking out the shape of a motionless figure lying just inside the interior of the building.

He went forward cautiously, gun in his right hand. His teeth clicked together when he recognized Bill Clayton. He dropped to one knee beside the man. Clayton was dead. A large patch of blood was spreading over his shirt-front. Shand gazed at his friend with blurring sight, and blinked rapidly as he forced himself to accept the situation. He got to his feet as Trask arrived, and the marshal groaned when he saw Clayton.

'Dead?' he enquired.

'Yeah.' Shand drew a deep breath. 'Did you recognize the rider who pulled out of here?'

'I didn't recognize him, but the horse sure looked familiar. He was splitting the breeze like there was no tomorrow.'

'Can I borrow your horse? I'll ride out after that bozo.'

'Sure. It's in a stall along there. I'll check out this business. Watch your step, Cole.'

Shand went into the stable and located the marshal's grey. He saddled up and led the animal outside, swung into the saddle and rode out fast after the fleeing rider. A sense of relief gripped him as he left Longhorn Crossing. He had felt constricted by the town and the instructions Frank Merrick had given him. He knew that the only way to fight the coming battle was by hitting HTR where it would do the most damage; at their end of track to the north. But he was aware that his orders precluded such direct action, and that placed him at a great disadvantage.

He noted the tracks of the fleeing horse and sent

the big grey forward at its best pace. His quarry was several hundred yards ahead and moving fast. Shand settled down to some serious riding and soon realized that he had a slight edge over the fleeing rider. He was better mounted, and Trask's horse was fresh and raring to go.

A glance at the position of the sun informed him that the afternoon was almost past. He checked the general direction his quarry was taking and realized that the man was riding towards the SWRR end of track. Urging the horse to greater effort, Shand lessened the distance separating him from the fleeing man and hammered on, wanting to get to grips. He was heartened by the sight of his quarry slowing, and excitement grew in his breast at the prospect of riding the man down.

Miles passed quickly under the fleeing hoofs of the big grey, and Shand began to overhaul the fugitive hand over fist. He reached for his pistol and cocked the weapon and, although at extreme range, triggered two shots that chased out the silence of the hot afternoon. Echoes filled his ears, and the next instant the killer's horse faltered in its stride before sprawling in a welter of jerking limbs. The animal cartwheeled, its rider vacating the saddle in a low arc, then both horse and man hit the ground in a crashing fall and all movement ceased.

Shand closed in with ready gun. The chips were down again and the game was hot and furious.

FOUR

Shand approached the fallen rider with his pistol in his right hand. Both horse and man were inert, and dust was floating from their impact with the hard ground. The man looked as if he had broken his neck. His head was lying at an unnatural angle. He was on his face with both arms outstretched, showing no further interest in Shand's activities. The horse was still alive, breathing torturously, snuffling in the dust, its eyes rolling wildly. Blood was showing on its neck where one of Shand's bullets had struck it.

He checked the horse first, and finished it off with a single shot through its brain. His eyes were narrowed and over-bright when he turned his attention to the man, whom he recognized as one of those he had interviewed earlier and turned down for a job. He could not remember the man's name and had not employed him purely on instinct. Now he was dead. Shand drew a pistol from the man's holster and checked it, finding that it had been fired recently.

A search of the man's clothing and saddle-bags revealed nothing, and Shand stood looking down at the body, wondering at the death of Bill Clayton. He looked around and saw nothing but empty range, with only the twin steel tracks of the railroad off to the left, leading to the SWRR construction camp. He turned back to his horse. As he swung into the saddle a bullet struck the ground within a yard of him and he heard the crack of a rifle shot.

The bullet was not near enough to be hostile, and Shand twisted in his saddle to see two riders coming over a ridge from the direction of end of track. One of them was waving a rifle, and Shand relaxed, recognizing the pair as Pat Eke and Tom Baldwin. He waited for them to arrive, and both men were smiling broadly as they reined in before him.

Eke was tall and lean, dark-haired, handsome, a man in his late twenties who had been a lawman in his youth. Baldwin was short and running to fat, fair-haired, in his early thirties. Both had worked with Shand for more than a year.

'Glad to see you back, Cole,' Eke greeted. 'We might get on the move again now, huh?'

'Looks like you've already made a fresh start,' Baldwin observed, eyeing the dead man.

'Have either of you seen him before?' Shand queried.

Baldwin shook his head instantly but Eke stepped down from his saddle and dropped to his haunches beside the body.

'I saw him three days ago at end of track,' Eke said at length. 'He was pestering Hank Belmont for a job. Hank told him to ride into town to see you.'

'I saw him today, and turned him down,' Shand

49

said. 'He left town later, after killing Bill Clayton.'

'Bill's dead?' Eke straightened, his expression harsh.

'Hell, there's no end to HTR's murdering ways.' Baldwin glanced around. 'Now you're back, Cole, how's about us riding over to their construction camp and taking it to pieces? We ain't never gonna beat them by just fighting off their attacks, and they've got to be wiped out before they nail us down.'

Shand explained the events that had occurred in town and both men were shocked. He told them they were to guard Poggin in the jail; neither man was pleased by the decision.

'Heck, you should have killed that skunk when you had the chance,' Eke said. 'It ain't good to stick a man like Poggin behind bars as if he's human. Cole, I reckon something bad could happen to Poggin if I take up guarding him.'

'They want to make an example of him,' Shand said, 'so you better guard him with your lives. Let's ride back to town and get organized. What's it like at end of track? Is Hank getting on with the job?'

'Sure thing.' Eke nodded. 'Nothing will stop Hank, come hell or high water. There've been one or two small incidents out there in the last week, but nothing to stop the work. Pinpricks, Hank called them.'

'Such as?' Shand demanded.

'Three days ago someone sneaked into rifle range and put some holes in the water-tank,' Baldwin said. 'It wasn't serious. Guards are riding the perimeter all the time, but it's impossible to stop those attacks.

50

Anyway, Luke Preston took a shot at the man, but he got away, hanging over his saddle. We've just checked the track all the way back from the camp to that ridge over there and found nothing wrong.'

'We'll check the rest of it back to town,' Shand decided. 'Let's get moving. I want to be in Longhorn Crossing by sundown.'

'What about this guy?' Eke asked.

'Leave him,' Shand decided. 'I'll send Joe Ivey out tomorrow with a wagon to collect him. We've got to play our game according to the law in future. Our activities are being watched closely by the bosses back East.'

They mounted and rode towards the railroad tracks. When they reached them, they turned left and headed east towards Longhorn Crossing. The range was undulating and rough. Shand glanced around repeatedly, checking their surroundings. They rode through a cutting in a low ridge and continued. Shand never ceased to marvel at the way the surveyors and graders overcame obstacles in their progress. Nothing ever stopped them. They spanned every low place and cut their way through high ground, driving on in as straight a line as Nature permitted.

'Say, there's movement ahead,' Baldwin said suddenly.

Shand peered ahead and saw three riders moving away from a trestle-bridge spanning a gorge. The riders had spotted them and were raising dust as they headed south-west.

'They look suspicious.' Shand pushed his horse

into a run. 'Go get 'em. I'll take a look at the span.'

'Be careful,' Eke warned. 'There's only one reason why they'd be here. They've probably set a dynamite charge under the trestle.'

Shand rode hard while Eke and Baldwin angled after the galloping riders. The gorge was ninety yards wide and sixty feet deep. He rode around a hill on his approach, and while he was out of sight of the span and behind the cover of the hill a terrific explosion rent the stillness and thunderous echoes rolled across country. Shand's ears were battered by the noise and debris from the explosion began to rain down around him – lengths of shattered wood from the trestle, and a long length of steel track that came whirling to earth only a few yards from him.

He saw a billowing cloud of black smoke rising rapidly into the bright sky. He moved into the open to rein up while the effects of the explosion diminished slowly. When the lethal shower subsided he urged the nervous horse forward until he was level with the span, then he reined in to gaze at the gaping hole that had been blown in the trestle and the tracks. Echoes were still grumbling away into the distance, as if reluctant to leave the scene of the disturbance.

A sigh escaped Shand. He was filled with anger at such a waste of effort and labour. A repair gang could replace the trestle and the tracks, but the war with HTR was so unnecessary. He heard the crackle of shots in the distance and wheeled his horse to ride fast along the tracks the three departing riders had left. His ears were still protesting at the man-made thunder that had wrecked the span, and in his mind a grim determination to hit HTR where it really hurt was beginning to take shape.

Shooting was hammering relentlessly when Shand rode in sight of the showdown that was taking place. The three strangers were hunkered down in cover, shooting at Eke and Baldwin as the two men worked their way in close. Shand did not hesitate. He circled to the right and stayed behind cover as he moved in. Eke spotted him and waved a hand in acknowledgement of his presence. Shand dismounted, drew his rifle from its boot, and hunted cover to join in the fight.

The three men were down in a pile of rocks and looked determined as they exchanged shots with Eke and Baldwin. Shand joined in and one of the trio turned to engage him. Bullets splattered against his cover and whined around him. He edged forward into a good position and returned fire steadily.

Shand saw a Stetson rise slightly above a rock and fired instantly, putting a slug into centre of the movement. The hat disappeared quickly, and then its owner pitched sideways from behind his cover and lay motionless in the open with arms outflung. A sigh gusted from Shand. He was becoming more and more disillusioned with the way the battle with HTR was going, realizing that his recent experiences, when he had been shot in the last showdown, had affected him adversely. He had not been aware of the fact until he found action again.

Had he lost his nerve? The question filtered through his mind as he watched for another target.

He did not feel scared. He was determined to do his job to the best of his considerable ability, as he had always done. So what was wrong with him? Something was sticking in his craw and he could not put a name to it. He tried to drive the distracting thoughts from his mind but found them too deeply entrenched to be dismissed.

Eke nailed a second man, and then he and Baldwin got up and rushed the rocks, shooting as they closed in. Shand arose and moved in quickly. When he reached the spot he found his two men covering the remaining man, who was dying with a bullet in his chest.

'I hoped to take him alive,' Eke said softly, 'but he didn't want that. From the sound of the explosion I reckon the span has gone, huh, Cole?'

'You can say that again.' Shand spoke harshly. 'You two get back to town as fast as you can and take these bodies with you. I'll ride to end of track and get a repair crew sent back. Don't forget your duties when you hit town. I expect an attempt will be made pretty soon to bust Poggin out of jail, and I want to see him still behind bars when I ride in. OK?'

'You can count on it,' Baldwin told him.

Shand helped them load the three bodies across their saddles, and when the grim little cavalcade set out for town he rode back to the wrecked trestle to assess the damage before heading westward to end of track. Evening was drawing on. The sun was well over in the western half of the sky and shadows were lengthening. When darkness came he made camp and rolled himself in his blankets, feeling exhausted both physically and mentally. He had returned to duty to find that nothing had changed in the two months he had been away. He still had it all to do, despite the sense of disquiet making its presence felt in his mind.

He was awake and ready to ride before the sun showed over the eastern horizon the next morning. He felt gaunt inside, and had to fight a personal battle to get his thoughts moving in the right channel. There was a strange reluctance governing him which tried to induce him to turn his back upon this job and ride off to seek a more peaceful existence far from this situation. Before the last showdown he had been ready to give his life in the course of his job, but the two months he had spent recuperating from his shoulder wound seemed to have left his mind scarred, and he struggled against a strange mood as he rode on to the construction camp.

It was mid-morning when he topped a rise and saw the SWRR end of track spread out before him. He reined in and gazed at the familiar sight. The work of laying rails was in full swing. Work routine in the construction camp started at sun-up and continued until dusk. The surveyors and graders were miles ahead of the camp, pushing steadily towards Indian Pass, their heavy work consisting of filling in ravines or cutting through high ground; blasting solid rock where necessary, building trestles across rivers and gorges, hammering tunnels through mountains, and cutting passes through ridges; all done mainly by human muscle-power.

The work crews regularly laid between two and five

miles of track each day, depending on the ground they were covering. Ahead of them the graders prepared the ground and pick-and-shovel men smoothed out undulations. All the work was co-ordinated, for the failure of one seemingly insignificant cog could bring the whole organization to a halt.

Shand was pleased by the signs of bustling activity as he looked around. A steam whistle sounded, sending echoes across the barren landscape. A railroad coach was standing on a small loop-line – the headquarters of the construction camp boss Hank Belmont, and Shand saw the big, powerful figure of Belmont standing near the coach, talking to several men gathered around him.

Flatcars loaded with rails and equipment were being shunted by a small work locomotive towards the end of the gleaming tracks. The cars stopped within half a mile of the railhead and the rails were loaded on to horse-drawn carts. Each cart went at a gallop to the end of track, where work-gangs were waiting to handle them.

A cart was being unloaded, the men working in groups of five; the first two taking hold of a 500-pound rail and moving forward while others stepped in behind them along the length of the rail until it was clear of the cart. They went forward at a run and dropped the rail, right side up, in place on the wooden ties set out on the prepared roadbed. The gangs averaged four rails a minute throughout the long hours of daylight, and each rail was secured to the ties with thirty spikes, each spike requiring just three blows to drive it home. There were 400 rails to a mile of track.

As he rode in Shand noted that the working men had rifles piled close to hand; he was pleased to see that his advice was being heeded. There had been three bad attacks on the camp in the past, and the workers were prepared to defend themselves while the troubleshooters took care of the more vulnerable surveyors and graders out ahead.

Men looked up from their work to greet Shand, some calling wishes for his welfare. He grinned and waved in return, a popular man who had the lives of these people in his hands. He was very much aware that if he ever made an error of judgement then someone could die. He rode towards the railroad coach and, as he approached, the group of men around Hank Belmont dispersed and hurried away about their business. The construction camp boss turned and waited for Shand to reach him, his leathery face set in harsh lines.

Hank Belmont was a man in his middle forties, short and heavily built, his massive frame covered by a wrinkled and stained blue store suit that had seen better days. He wore a black derby hat, the brim of which was low over his eyes, and his feet were encased in heavy leather work boots that had reinforced toecaps. His eyes were blue and far-seeing, and he permitted a smile to touch his lips, which were almost hidden behind a bushy black moustache. Shand knew the camp boss as a man who suffered mental disquiet from the immeasurable tensions of his perilous job.

'It's good to see you back in harness, Cole,'

Belmont greeted in a low-pitched voice. 'With you here we might be able to get on with the job without a lot of time-wasting ideas and shilly-shallying being pitched at us from head office. I've had it up to the back teeth, I can tell you, and I reckon I won't take much more of it. If I get another piece of foolish advice from Frank Merrick I'll quit cold and he can come out here, take over, and try to handle the job with all the handicaps they're piling on me.'

'I got some bad news for you, Hank,' Shand interrupted the other's complaint and explained the events that had occurred the previous day.

Belmont gazed at Shand with horror dawning in his pale eyes, then he smashed his left fist into his calloused right palm.

'I knew it!' he rasped. 'I've had the feeling that another dirty campaign was about to start. All that claptrap from head office about not using violence to solve our problems is just so much hot air. I told Merrick to invite the bosses to come to end of track and see for themselves what it's like to push this line west with so much violence coming at us.'

'Frank says to carry on in the same old way and he'll keep those bozos back East from falling on our necks.'

'Give me a couple of minutes,' Belmont interrupted. 'I need to get the repair gang started back to the blown trestle. I hope you can stop these attacks on us, Cole. We're working flat out, and I don't need this kind of setback.'

Shand nodded and watched Belmont hurry across to a group of men moving the small loop-line nearer to end of track. Shand watched, shaking his head and wondering how he was going to be able to oversee the whole area, aware that it was an impossible task to cover every yard of the line. Their competitors knew it also, and the argument for attacking HTR's construction camp and putting it out of business was becoming more and more attractive. Shand could see no alternative, and knew it would have to be done before they could hope to win through.

Belmont came back to Shand, shaking his head, filled with concern about what had to be done.

'I thought things have been too quiet since that last bust-up,' he said. 'I'll have to send some of your troubleshooters back with the repair gang. I need another supply train out from Longhorn Crossing so the line has got to be up and running again as soon as possible. We're getting short of vital stock. Why don't you take your boys and hit HTR's construction camp? The last report I got about their progress placed them about five miles east of Clear Creek. They're still well behind us, but with the delays we're getting, I can't guarantee to be at Indian Pass before them.'

'Something drastic will have to be done,' Shand agreed. 'I'll have another talk with Frank when I get back to Longhorn Crossing, and I'll push for a big strike at HTR.'

'I'd like to stand and chat with you.' Belmont's gaze was never still, flickering around his domain, checking that his workers were doing their utmost. 'Let me know what Frank says about hitting HTR. Some of my work gangs wanta be on that, if it comes about. I've promised them a day off from work to take part, if it happens.'

'I'll see what I can arrange. I'll ride the train back to where the trestle is down and then hoof it back to town.'

Belmont nodded and hurried away, shouting at a group of workers nearby. Shand watched for a moment and then rode across to where big Buck Ryan, the leader of the repair work-gang, was urging his workers to load flatcars with the supplies they would need at the broken trestle. The big Irishman was stripped to the waist, working prodigiously as he urged his crew to great effort. He paused when Shand reached him, and grinned, his fist-battered face dripping sweat.

'I'll ride back with you as far as you're going, Buck, then head for town. You've got a big job on your hands.'

'Haven't I always?' Ryan grinned, exposing broken front teeth. 'I'll need some of your troubleshooting buckos to guard my men while they're working.'

'I'll round them up right now.' Shand dismounted and trailed his reins. He looked around the sprawling camp, spotted some faces he knew, and summoned six of his crew who were acting as guards, placing one, Jake Denver, in command of the detachment. They needed little in the way of instruction for they were experienced men.

The repair train was not ready to leave until three hours after Shand had ridden into the camp. Fifty men swarmed around it like a colony of ants, loading timber for the trestle, rails, bolts, fishplates, and all the other equipment needed for repairs. A boxcar for the horses of the troubleshooters was added and the animals were loaded. Finally, the train pulled out, heading back along the line, and Shand stood in the doorway of the boxcar to take a last look at the labours of the construction gang toiling with the mighty task of pushing new rails to the mouth of the distant Indian Pass.

It was around the middle of the afternoon when the repair gang descended upon the broken trestle like a swarm of locusts, and by the time Shand had unloaded his horse from the boxcar and was ready to ride out they were already hard at work, removing broken timbers from the shattered ruin and unloading replacements from the train. Shand gave final instructions to his troubleshooters and then rode off along the line towards Longhorn Crossing, determined to force the issue with Frank Merrick. They had to make a new approach to the situation. HTR had called the shots for too long. SWRR had to change its tactics or lose the race to Indian Pass. It was as simple as that. They had to fight fire with fire or go under.

FIVE

Night fell as Shand rode into Longhorn Crossing. The heat of the long day was dissipating as shadows crept insidiously into the town. Yellow lamplight was showing in windows, and he could hear the sound of strident piano music echoing along the wide street. He rode into the stable and took care of Ben Trask's horse, then walked along the sidewalk to the jail to check on the situation before considering his own needs.

The door of the law office was bolted, and Shand hammered on the sun-warped panels. There was a light in the office and, while he awaited a reply, Shand hoped his men were on duty as he had directed. Then Pat Eke's harsh voice called a challenge from behind the heavy door, and Shand replied. Eke opened the door abruptly, and Shand found himself looking into the black muzzle of a deadly pistol.

'Hi, Cole.' Eke lowered his pistol, a grin on his face. 'Glad to see you back. Nothing to report this end. Poggin is still snug in his cell, and he ain't happy with me and Baldwin living here so I reckon he's still got hopes of being busted out. I'll be glad when they hang him. I can't stand the sound of his voice.'

'That's good news,' Shand commented. 'You're keeping an eye on the town as well, huh?'

'Sure. There'll be other HTR men showing up, you can bet. We're covering the job all ways to the middle. There ain't a mouse can move around town without us seeing it. You better drop in on Merrick before you do anything else. He was working himself into a big sweat around town this afternoon, and looked in here several times, hoping to find you around. From what he said I got a feeling you're gonna get the chance of hitting HTR where it hurts, and I'm hoping my instincts aren't playing me for a fool.'

'That sounds promising.' Shand grinned. 'I'll see him right away. Stay on your toes, Pat. Tell Ben I'll get around to seeing him later.'

Eke closed and bolted the door of the office as Shand turned and then went along the sidewalk in the direction of the house where Frank Merrick lived close to the rail depot with his wife Ann. He passed the Red Steer saloon and peered in over the batwings, his keen gaze searching the faces of the men inside. Satisfied that all was well he went on, but turned aside as he reached the restaurant. He entered the dining-room, aware that his nagging hunger would have to be assuaged before he could settle to further duty.

Abby Swain was standing by the door to the kitchen, keeping an eye on her diners. The big room was almost filled to capacity, and Shand walked to

Abby's side, noting the way the woman's face brightened when her eyes latched on to his big figure.

'Cole, I'm glad to see you! Come on into the back room and I'll get you some food. I need to talk to you, and when I heard you'd left town last night I didn't think you'd be back this side of Christmas. This is a stroke of luck. Are you hungry? I got a big steak just waiting for your attention.'

'Have you ever known me to come in here when I ain't hungry?' he countered with a grin. 'But I don't have much time to spare, Abby. I need to eat, and then I got to see Frank. He's been asking around town for me, and there's always something stirring when he's on the prod.'

He followed Abby into the back room and she continued on into the kitchen. Shane sat down at the table and tried to relax. He removed his hat and pressed his fingers against his eyes. There was a nagging pain in the scar of the bullet wound in his left shoulder. When Abby brought a filled plate and set it before him he began to eat. He hardly paid any attention to the food he shovelled into his mouth beyond registering that it was good and well cooked. Abby watched him for some moments, and then shook her head and departed. She returned with coffee as he finished the meal.

'It's good to see you doing justice to my food.' Abby poured two cups of coffee and sat down opposite Shand to drink one of them.

'What do you wanta talk to me about, Abby?' he cut in. 'Is it important? I got to be running along.'

'Sure it's important! I wouldn't be bothering you if

it wasn't. And you can just sit there for a couple of minutes to take a breather while your meal goes down. Cole, I hear a lot of gossip in the course of a day, and an interesting snippet came to me when Charles Fenton and Hiram Courtney were in around noon. Fenton said he was in a hurry because he had an appointment with a Henry Padlow this afternoon. That's all I heard, but the name he mentioned jogged my memory. A Henry Padlow runs a district for HTR. Could it be the same man, and if it is, what's he doing in Longhorn Crossing? This is a SWRR town.'

'Padlow!' Shand frowned. 'He is the man running the fight against us. I don't think he'd show his face around here. And what would he want with Fenton? That banker has always got his eyes on his profit margins, but he wouldn't do business with the enemy, or would he? If you can't trust the banker then who can you put your faith in?'

'That's what I've been asking myself.' Abby's fleshy face wore a big frown. 'In my book, Fenton is a man to be trusted. Courtney is the one I wouldn't trust any further than I could throw him. For a lawyer, he's got an unfortunate face with those snake-eyes of his.'

Shand got to his feet. 'I'd better make tracks,' he said. 'Thanks for the meal, Abby. That steak was worth waiting all day for.'

'Come back again soon, Cole,' she replied. 'Barbara is feeling lonely already, and I hope you can pay her some interest; a fine, upstanding young man like you. Apart from you, there ain't a man around here I'd give houseroom to when it comes to Barbara's interests.'

'Hey, Abby, I ain't got time to socialize, and you know it,' Shand protested. 'There's a big showdown coming, and I'd better be ready to face it or we'll take a beating. I'll see you around, huh?'

He left the restaurant and hurried along the street towards Frank Merrick's house. A faint noise reached his ears as he passed an alley-mouth and he turned instantly, his pistol leaping into his hand.

'Who's there?' he demanded, cocking his gun.

'Hold it, Cole, It's Pete Howlett.' A dark figure moved forward out of the darkness of the alley.

'You don't oughta sneak up on me like that, Pete,' Shand said quickly. 'It's bad for my nerves.'

'Sorry. I saw you going into the eating-house and I didn't want to be seen talking to you. Frank Merrick set me to watching the banker's house this afternoon. A man named Padlow was in town to see Fenton. He left just after sundown. I reported to Merrick, who told me to watch out for you.'

'I'm on my way to see Frank now. Did you learn anything about Padlow?'

'Nope. I saw that him and Fenton were on good-friend terms, and they looked over some papers the lawyer brought to them. Padlow took a copy of the papers with him when he left.'

'How did Padlow leave town?' Shand asked.

'He caught the train to El Paso.'

'I'd better see Frank. Wait around for me, Pete. Get yourself a drink in the Red Steer. I'll see you there shortly.'

'Sure thing. How's it going at end of track? I talked to Eke when he came into town. He was full of the attack on that trestle. Looks like the supply train ain't goin' through tomorrow morning.'

'The supplies will go through,' Shand replied, and went on.

Frank Merrick had just finished his supper and was smoking his customary after-dinner pipe when Shand walked in on him.

'This is one of those times when I wish you could be in several places at once, Cole,' he greeted.

'If you're talking about Padlow's visit, I already heard about it,' Shand replied. 'Why didn't you stop him getting on the train to El Paso? You should have gotten a look at those papers he took from Fenton.'

'I've wired our office in El Paso and someone will lift the papers off Padlow when he gets there.' Merrick's tone was harsh and his eyes glinted. 'We'll get to know what he was cooking up with Fenton.'

'Do you want me to ask Fenton what was going on?' A trace of eagerness tinged Shand's tone.

'Not until we know what those papers are about. I got a feeling it might have to do with the new approach our head office people were talking about. They're insisting on negotiation, not confrontation.'

'The soft approach!' Shand grinned. 'What will they make of the attack on our trestle yesterday?'

'I doubt it will change anything. You got the repair job in hand?'

'Sure. It'll be repaired, but Hank is getting low on supplies.'

'The supply train will run to the wrecked trestle

and everything will have to be manhandled across the gap to a work train on the far side. I'm sending a big work-crew with the train, and the essential stuff should reach Henry without too much delay. We've had worse jobs than this, Cole. The thing is, I'm thinking of retaliating against HTR. I can't order you to handle it, but if something big should hit HTR I reckon it would be rough justice against them, and it's overdue.'

'It's not like you to resort to extreme measures, Frank. You've always had your foot on the soft pedal. I can take a bunch of men over to HTR with no trouble and hit them where it hurts most, but what happens when the news gets out? You'll deny ordering the attack, and I'll get fired for going against new company policy – talk not fight.'

'I think I can smooth that over when we come to it.' Determination sounded in Merrick's harsh voice. 'Where would you hit HTR to give them a real body blow?'

'The trestle they got spanning Devil's Gorge. It's ten times bigger than the trestle we lost yesterday. HTR had a helluva job spanning that gorge last year, and that's the obvious place to hit them. Then I'd blow up every bit of rolling stock and supply dump they got between the gorge and their end of track. That'll stop them dead for months. It's what I've had in mind for a long time.'

'Devil's Gorge will be heavily guarded. You'd need to take most of our troubleshooting crew. How many men can you muster?'

'Twenty should turn the trick.'

'OK. So start making your plans, but don't do anything until we know what Padlow has got in those papers Fenton gave him.' Merrick sighed heavily and shook his head as he considered. 'I reckon we'll both lose our jobs if we have to act,' he opined.

Shand departed immediately, but paused at the door, his face set in harsh lines as he looked at Merrick.

'I reckon there are a number of HTR spies in town,' he said softly. 'I'd better get explosives from our end of track. Can I tell Hank Belmont about this?'

'Sure. If we can't trust Hank then we can't trust anyone. Send your raiding party to end of track and pick them up there when you're ready to go, but you'd better stick around town until we hear from El Paso about Padlow.'

Shand nodded and went out into the night. He paused on the sidewalk and looked around into the shadows, sensing an air of hostility lying over the town. Suddenly the situation was in danger of exploding in his face, and he knew he had better be ready for anything. He went along to the saloon and entered to find Pete Howlett leaning against the bar, an untouched drink before him.

'What's worrying you, Pete?' Shand signalled to the tender for a beer, which came sliding along the bar with uncanny accuracy. Harper came for the money, and leaned forward conspiratorially to speak in an undertone.

'What's going on, Cole?' he demanded. 'This place is dead and ready to be buried. Where is everyone? We'll be out of business if it goes on like this.'

'Our men are probably getting ready to leave for end of track in the morning,' Shand replied. 'I wouldn't know what HTR's spies are doing.' He glanced sideways at Howlett. 'Do you know any of them by sight, Pete?'

'Yeah, several, and they ain't showing themselves tonight. That is what's worrying me. They must be planning something, and we need an edge to beat them. I've been around town a couple of times, checking the places where they usually hang out when they ain't in here, but there's no sign of them, and I'm sure they haven't pulled out.'

'Did Padlow contact any of them while he was here?' Shand asked.

'Not while I was watching him.' Howlett shook his head. 'What do we do, Cole?'

'We wait, and be ready for any trouble that starts,' Shand replied firmly.

He picked up his beer and drank deeply. As he set the glass back on the bar a fusillade of shots smashed the silence with heart-stopping suddenness. Shand froze for one interminable second before reacting, and then turned instantly to run to the batwings, drawing his pistol as he moved. Pete Howlett followed a couple of paces behind.

The shooting continued in one long roll of thunder, and Shand estimated that a dozen guns were in action. He shouldered through the batwings, and two pistols fired at him from the darkness across the street, splitting the dense shadows with long spurts of reddish flame. A slug tore through the crown of his

Stetson and thudded into the front wall of the saloon; a second one stung the lobe of his right ear. He hurled himself flat on the sidewalk, his pistol spouting flame and hot lead in quick reply.

Howlett emerged from the saloon and fell over Shand, bouncing on the edge of the sidewalk before rolling into the dust of the street. Shand thought Howlett had been hit, but the man started shooting immediately, and the guns opposite fell silent. Shand peered along the street as he regained his feet. Guns were flashing from several points around the jail, and answering fire was stabbing from the front windows of the law office. Heavy echoes growled menacingly across the darkened town.

Howlett joined Shand, his fingers busy reloading his gun.

'We know where they are now,' Howlett shouted. 'Let's go get them.'

Shand was already moving along the sidewalk, noting the positions of the guns shooting into the office. He saw four dim figures suddenly run across the street towards the front door of the jail, shooting as they moved, and he triggered his pistol rapidly. The gunflashes dazzled his gaze and he blinked rapidly. A gun started shooting at him from across the street. He ducked and sent two probing shots at the gunflash. Howlett uttered a cry and fell headlong into the dust. Shand kept moving, his eyes mere slits as he peered through shadows and drifting gunsmoke.

Two more guns directed a stream of lead in Shand's direction and he threw himself to the left across the sidewalk and into a nearby alley, followed by the ominous sounds of slugs thudding into the woodwork around him. He drew a deep breath and returned fire, aiming for gunflashes, and the volume of fire against him slackened gradually.

He peered towards the jail and saw a number of dark figures crowding together around the door of the office. Someone was shooting in through the big front window. Shand reloaded his smoking gun and turned it loose again, aiming for the man doing the shooting. He saw several figures running for cover, but the door of the office was open now and all resistance against the attackers had apparently ceased.

Shand left the alley and ran across the street to narrow his angle of fire on the jail. He saw two men coming out of an alley further along the street, leading several horses towards the law office. He shot one of the men and four horses went galloping away. The second man turned and headed for the nearest alley, leading his horses, and Shand was forced to hold his fire. He stepped into an alley almost opposite the jail and reloaded his pistol.

The next instant a group of some half-dozen men emerged from the law office and ran to where the horses were being held in cover. Shand recognized the big figure of Nat Poggin in their midst and cut loose, emptying his pistol into the thick of the group. He saw Poggin stagger and then fall, but someone bent over the man and dragged him upright. By the time Shand had reloaded yet again there was no one in sight. As the echoes of the shooting faded he caught the sound of receding hoofs pounding away along the alley.

An uneasy silence settled quickly as Shand went towards the law office. His ears were ringing from the shooting. He held his gun levelled and ready for action. He went in through the open front door and saw Pat Eke lying on the floor in a corner, unconscious but not dead. Eke's shirt-front had two red splotches high in the chest.

Shand moved to the open door of the cell block and peered inside. Ben Trask was sitting in front of a cell, his legs stretched out before him and his back against the bars. He was barely conscious, with blood spreading in a patch on the right side of his chest. Tom Baldwin was lying on his face nearby, his arms outstretched, and he was dead. Shand bent over Trask and spoke reassuringly. The town marshal did not reply.

Shand went back to the street. Townsmen were showing themselves now, coming forward cautiously, and Shand called to them, telling one of them to fetch Doc Gilroy and others to get lanterns and check out the street for all the men who had been shot. He went along the sidewalk to the alley into which the attackers had fled, hoping to find the body of Nat Poggin somewhere around, but there was no sign of the hardcase. He had vanished with the departing horses.

Pete Howlett came staggering towards Shand, and dropped to his knees as his strength failed. There was blood on his shirt-front, and Shand knelt to examine Howlett, who slid full length on the sidewalk and lay breathing heavily. A townsman approached with a lantern and held it high over Howlett, who was unconscious. Shand opened Howlett's shirt to reveal a bullet hole below the right shoulder.

'Stay with him and do what you can to stop the bleeding,' Shand directed, yawning to unblock the pressure in his ears. 'I'll get the doc here pronto.'

The townsman set down the lantern and dropped to his knees beside the wounded man.

Doc Gilroy was already approaching the law office, medical bag in hand, and quickly assumed control of the situation. Shand followed him into the office. The doc wasted no time. Four of the townsmen crowding around the door of the office were instructed to carry Pat Eke to the medical office, and Ben Trask followed moments later. Tom Baldwin was pronounced dead, and Shand was grim-faced as he led Gilroy out to where Pete Howlett was lying.

'I've done what I can to stop the bleeding, Doc,' said the townsman tending Howlett. 'I don't think his life is in danger.'

Gilroy dropped to his knees and examined Howlett's wound. He arose and signalled to some of the crowding townsmen to convey Howlett to his office.

'There are at least eight HTR gunnies lying around the street,' Shand observed.

'I make no distinction between good and bad men,' Gilroy replied. 'You can leave this side of the job to me, Cole. I am thankful that I managed to eat my meal before the shooting started. It was considerate of you to hold your fire. Is there likely to be any more shooting before morning?'

'I hope so.' Shand smiled grimly. 'Nat Poggin was busted out of jail and I want to get him. Take care of my men before handling any who work for HTR.'

'You don't have to tell me my job,' Gilroy retorted.

Frank Merrick approached Shand, and was clearly displeased when he learned of Poggin's escape. He glanced around the dim street, shaking his head and sighing.

'Why are you standing around here, Cole?' he demanded. 'You should be forking your bronc and tracking down that killer instead of wasting time.'

'If you can see tracks in the dark then you'd better ride out after him yourself,' Shand replied testily. 'Me, I'm gonna have to wait for sun-up, and I'll get Poggin before he can cause any more trouble. I'll bring him in alive if I can or dead if I have to. Get off my back, Frank. I don't need your spurs in my flanks. You'd better report to those faceless wonders back East that HTR ain't keen on settling by negotiation, and I'll be interested in their reply when I get back toting Poggin face down across his saddle.'

Merrick grunted and stalked off. Shand gazed after him, his thoughts churning. The smell of gun smoke lingering in his nostrils filled him with an inner conflict, and he was aware that his mental attitude was not as it should be. Since the last showdown he was reluctant to throw himself whole-heartedly into the job. He wondered again if he was losing his nerve, then shrugged and went along the street to the saloon for a drink to erase the stink of action from his system.

Later he went along to Doc Gilroy's office to check

on Ben Trask, Eke and Howlett. The town marshal was unconscious and, in the doctor's opinion, would probably die before sun-up. Gilroy expected Pat Eke to survive, but he would have a tough job pulling through. Pete Howlett was a borderline case, and if he survived the next three days then there was a good chance he would eventually make it.

Shand was downcast as he left Gilroy's office. He walked along the main street to the edge of town and stood gazing into the dense shadows of the rough terrain stretching away to the distant Sierra Madre Mountains. His thoughts were swift as he tried to regain the mental fire that had attended him previously, but his determination was sadly depleted. Perhaps he needed another week before returning to the job, but he realized that the job would not wait for him. He was caught up in the thick of it again, and could only go forward to face what awaited him in the uncertain future.

He turned and retraced his steps, intending to seek his bed. He usually stayed at Frank Merrick's house when he was in town, but felt strangely reluctant to make further contact with the man who had brought him up as a son. He decided to bed down in the hayloft over the livery stable, and approached the building silently, his thoughts remote. A lantern was suspended from a nail over the wide doorway, and Shand entered into its circle of feeble light before realizing the danger of exposing himself. He lunged to the left, and heard the menacing hiss of a thrown knife even as he moved, then the heavy thud as the point of a deadly blade hit the thick wooden door beside his head.

Shand dropped to the ground, his holstered gun seeming to leap into his hand, cursing himself for a fool as he spotted swift movement in the surrounding darkness. He tilted the muzzle of his gun upwards and sent a shot into the lamp, extinguishing it as he rolled quickly to his right. Then the night was punctuated by gunfire and bullets splintered the door at his back as he moved fast to evade the trap that had been set for him.

SIX

A slug plucked at the sleeve of Shand's jacket just above the elbow, branding his flesh with fiery pain. He triggered his pistol, teeth clenched and muscles bunched, shooting at the gunflashes that split the darkness with deadly intensity. Three guns were shooting at him and he returned fire with grim determination, his eyes narrowed against the alternating extremes of flashing light and darkness. Gun echoes strung out across the town in quick succession, hammering and growling.

Shand flinched as a slug of hot lead tugged at his hat-brim in passing, and fired two quick shots at the gun flash that flared from behind an old wagon-bed off to the right. He fancied he had scored a hit, and when the pistol there did not maintain its shooting he twisted around to take on the remaining two ambushers. For some minutes lead whined through the darkness, until someone whistled in a low tone and the shooting stopped abruptly.

Echoes faded slowly and silence returned. Shand pushed himself to one knee and paused to thumb fresh shells into his pistol. He looked around, but now an uneasy silence reigned and there was no movement anywhere. Then he heard the sound of hoof-beats start up out there in the night before receding swiftly into the distance.

Shand pushed himself to his feet and holstered his gun. He stood with his back against the front wall of the stable and looked around, his gaze probing the surrounding shadows. His pulses were fast-beating, his heart pounding heavily. He was satisfied that the ambushers had fled, and a sigh escaped him as he went on into the stable and climbed into the hayloft, almost overcome by exhaustion.

He picked a spot in a pile of hay, settled down quickly and, despite his tension, fell sleep almost immediately. He lay motionless until the grey light of dawn filtered into the loft.

The sun was showing above the eastern horizon when Shand left the stable, and the first thing he saw when he looked around was a pair of booted feet sticking out from behind the derelict wagon-bed. He went across and peered down at a man lying stiff and cold on his back, his arms outflung carelessly. The man's bearded face was bloodied, and there was a bullet hole in his forehead. Shand gazed unemotionally at the corpse, thinking the dead face looked slightly familiar. He recalled seeing the man the year before, during a HTR raid on the construction camp, and stifled a sigh as he turned away.

He went along the street to the restaurant, and met Frank Merrick at the door.

'I was wondering why you didn't sleep in your bed

last night,' Merrick said. 'Were you involved in that shooting I heard?'

Shand explained and Merrick shook his head.

'It's always HTR causing trouble,' he said. 'I'm meeting with the town council this morning. They're concerned by all the trouble we're bringing in, and there's talk of a crackdown on us. We may have to move our headquarters out of town, and another marshal will hold us responsible for the peace.'

'It's about time the county sheriff put a deputy in here to keep an eye on things,' Shand observed. 'They can't throw us out. We're doing the town a service by fighting HTR. I'm gonna have breakfast, and then I'll pick up Poggin's trail and run him to earth.'

'I think there are more important things for you to do, Cole. Poggin can't do much now. We need to get ourselves organized to get our people into Indian Pass without too much trouble. Poggin is incidental. Just bear in mind that you should shoot him dead if you ever run across him.'

'You're the boss.' Shand shrugged. 'What do you want me to do?'

'I'm working on that. Give me an hour or so. I'm waiting on a message from head office before I finally decide what should be done. By the way, I had a wire from El Paso about Henry Padlow's visit here yesterday. Padlow's brief-case was lifted from him when he reached El Paso, but there were no papers in it linking him with Fenton.'

'Then I'd better see Fenton and talk to him about

Padlow,' Shand said softly.

'No.' Merrick shook his head. 'You can't rough up a banker and get away with it. Let it go for now. Prepare yourself for action. Report to my office in the rail depot in about two hours and I should be in a position to rough out our future campaign. Meanwhile, keep alert. It looks like HTR mean to put you out of business.'

'They can try,' Shand responded.

He went into the restaurant and Merrick turned away. Abby Swain came forward to greet Shand, her fleshy face exhibiting a troubled expression.

'It hasn't taken you long to get back into the thick of it, Cole,' she observed. 'I suppose you were mixed up in that shooting last night.' She took hold of his left wrist and examined the patch of dried blood surrounding the bullet tear in his shirt just above the left elbow. 'Come into my back room. I don't want you sitting out here in full view. Some of my diners are concerned about being near you, what with all the shooting you're attracting.'

Shand grimaced and followed Abby into the back room. He was pleased to see Barbara Madden seated at the table there, eating breakfast, and his pulses quickened when she smiled up at him.

'Good morning,' he greeted, and the harsh lines of his set expression faded as he smiled.

'Good morning,' she replied.

'I had a diner in for breakfast whom I knew in the old days back in Texas,' Abby cut in, and the degree of gravity in her voice caught and held Shand's attention. 'From what he was saying, I reckon he's going

81

to throw a lot of trouble your way, Cole.'

'Trouble?' Shand was jerked back to full alertness. 'Tell me about it.'

'I ain't seen Simp Rawley in a coon's age. His line of business is entertainment. He owns saloons and dance-halls all over the Southern states, and he talked of setting up a canvas saloon out to Kemp's Post for your construction workers. Ain't you got some kind of a rule against that sort of thing?'

Shand frowned. Kemp's Post was a trading post some twenty miles ahead of the present construction camp, and the railroad would drive rails within three miles of it on the way to Indian Pass.

'There's no law against it, but we would take a pretty dim view of anything that enticed workers away from their jobs.' Shand's eyes glinted. 'It's been tried before at other railroad construction camps, but they generally wind up out of business in a matter of hours. Where is Rawley? I've heard of him but never met him. I'd better get acquainted with him before I do anything else.'

He paused in the act of sitting down at the table. Abby placed a big hand on his shoulder and pushed him into the seat.

'You'll need your breakfast before you start chasing up railroad work,' she said determinedly. 'Rawley left town last night. He was in such an all-fired hurry that I thought his tail was on fire. Just sit and relax, Cole. You'll find Rawley at Kemp's Post in the next few days. From what he said, I reckon Henry Padlow had something to do with his decision to buck your railroad. In future you've got to expect a load of trouble that's different from anything you've had in the past. HTR are getting smarter the nearer your people lay rails to Indian Pass. I never thought I'd see the day when this town would rear up against the railroad, but all the trouble you're attracting has turned the trick.'

'So Frank told me.' Shand sighed and shook his head. 'Thanks for the news, Abby. I can't wait to set eyes on Rawley. Now, I can spare about five minutes for breakfast before I have to get moving.'

'Take your time.' Abby turned and waddled into her kitchen, returning moments later with a large plate of hot food which she placed before Shand.

He began to eat hungrily, and Abby fetched a coffee-pot from the kitchen. He was aware that Barbara watched his every movement, and her appearance pleased him, but his attention was on his job and he had no time for pleasantries or social graces. He scraped his plate clean and drank two cups of coffee before the girl finished eating her own breakfast. Then he pushed back his chair and got to his feet.

'That sure was a breakfast and a half,' he told Abby, who was standing in the background watching him with an indulgent smile on her face. 'You spoil me, Abby.'

'Go on with you, and watch your step out there, Cole. It's gonna get mighty rough.'

'Thanks for the information. I reckon my job will keep me out of town for a while so it should be quiet around here for a spell. See you when I get back.'

He left the restaurant and went along to the rail

depot to Merrick's office. Merrick was already at his desk, scanning a sheaf of paperwork. Shand explained about Simp Rawley. Merrick leaned back in his seat and heaved a long sigh.

'So that's what Padlow was doing here!' he mused. 'I reckon HTR are beginning to scrape the barrel for fresh ideas. It proves we're beating them in a straight fight. You better get out to Kemp's Post and warn Rawley off. Don't give him an inch. If you make it plain that there'll be no profit in what he's planning he'll change his mind about horning in.'

'I'll peg him out in the sun to dry if you want,' Shand said. 'I'll try and pick up Poggin's trail when I ride out.'

'You've got a thing about that killer.' Merrick shook his head. 'I told you he ain't that important. Concentrate on the bigger problems, Cole; that's an order.'

'Sure. I'll keep moving. See you later. If you want to contact me then leave a message at end of track. I'll be operating from there for the next week or so.'

He departed and walked along the street to Doc Gilroy's house.

'How are my wounded men?' he enquired when the doctor answered his knock at the door.

Gilroy looked as if he had been awake half the night. He stifled a yawn and blinked his pale eyes before sighing heavily.

'All well as can be expected. Ben Trask is dying slowly, and Eke is in a poor way, but Howlett ain't so badly hurt. They'll both need a lot of time to recover. I was about to have breakfast. Have you eaten yet?'

'Yeah. I'm riding out to end of track now. Things should be quieter when I'm not around. See you later, Doc.'

'I'll keep my fingers crossed that I don't have to see you professionally,' Gilroy replied.

Shand was thoughtful as he went to the stable. He saddled up Ben Trask's horse and rode back to the alley which Poggin and the men who had busted him out of jail had entered. In the cold light of morning he noted tracks and followed them. They led him across the back lots and west out of town; six riders moving fast and apparently with a definite destination in mind.

The tracks appeared to be heading towards end of track, and Shand was satisfied as he followed resolutely, aware that he had a thing in his mind about Nat Poggin. The hardcase had caused the deaths of several of his men and he meant to exact vengeance. He would not be able to rest until Poggin had paid the ultimate price for his murderous attacks on the railroad.

Three miles out of town the hoof-prints he was following veered away from the railroad tracks that were gleaming in the sunlight. Shand reined in and gazed in the direction Poggin had taken. It was in him to ignore Merrick's orders and take out after Poggin, but he fought down the urge and went on towards end of track. He expected Poggin to resume his attacks on the railroad, so their trails would inevitably cross again. He found comfort in that thought and rode steadily until he reached the scene of the wrecked trestle.

Repair work was in full swing. Some fifty men were swarming around the site like an army of ants. The repair gang was labouring at clearing the broken trestle and a gang of men was unloading the supply train that had come out from Longhorn Crossing – manhandling everything across the gap in the line to a string of flat cars that had been pushed back from end of track. Shand noted that a number of guards were alert around the area and checked with them before riding on. There had been no further trouble at the site.

It was mid-afternoon when he reached end of track, and the scene that awaited him was one of peacefulness. Work was going on at the usual fast pace and only the sounds of an engine and horses at work broke the brooding silence. He rode in and headed for Hank Belmont's coach. The camp boss appeared on the steps as Shand reined in and stepped down from his saddle.

'Anything wrong?' Belmont demanded suspiciously.

Shand explained the incidents that had taken place in town, and Belmont's expression hardened when he heard about Simp Rawley's arrival in Longhorn Crossing.

'Hey, I know that bozo,' he declared. 'He caused a lot of disruption for Union Pacific while I was working with them. The 'rust-eaters' flocked into Rawley's saloon instead of working, and schedules became non-existent until the troubleshooters ousted Rawley. I'm kind of surprised he's showed up here. He always seemed like a man who could learn from his mistakes, and he sure took a beating the last time he tried this trick. Someone must be paying him high stakes to try it again.'

'That's what I'm thinking,' Shand mused. 'I heard that Henry Padlow was in town a couple of days ago. He's bossing HTR's troubleshooters, so he might have been setting this up.'

'You'd better check out Kemp's Post right away, and if Rawley is putting up a tent there then you'll have to deal with it before he gets settled in. And don't make the mistake of riding in there alone, Cole. You'll need an army to crack Rawley's set-up.'

'I'm heading out that way right now,' Shand said.

He remounted, rode on to the end of track, then paused for a moment to watch the work-gangs manhandling lengths of rail into position. He marvelled at the speed and apparent ease attained by the 'rust-eaters', and dragged himself away to continue along the roadbed that had been levelled by the graders.

Shand was not happy with the general situation or the way it was evolving. To his way of thinking it was wrong to be on the defensive. To win through in this particular deal they had to strike their competitors a telling blow, and his fighting instincts warned that now was the logical moment to deliver it. But apparently his superiors were loath to give the order that would bring success, and Shand was aware that they might very well lose this war even with success in sight. He wondered if he could stretch his orders to cover what he knew was the sensible thing to do.

When he topped a ridge and saw Kemp's Post before him he reined back below the skyline, dismounted and trailed his reins, then bellied up a slope until he could observe the peaceful scene, which he had seen many times before. He studied the single-storey building that sprawled untidily beside a water-hole and noted six horses in a rope corral to the left of the Post. A frown flickered across his face when he saw five big wagons pulled up behind the store, which were being unloaded by a dozen men. There seemed to be a large volume of goods for such a small trading post, and he guessed that Rawley's tent saloon had already arrived.

He knew Abe Kemp as a tough businessman with a brusque manner, and guessed that he would be in on any deal that had been arranged to entice the railroad workers from their job. He went back to his horse and circled the Post, staying out of sight until he was at the rear, where he dismounted and knee-hobbled his horse in a dry wash. He sneaked along the gully until he was twenty yards from the wagons, and did not need to study the scene long before he ascertained that the wagons were not supplying the store.

A vast canvas tent had been spread out flat on the ground and men were driving posts into position within the area that had been cleared and flattened to receive it. There were several women present, helping to unload cases from some of the wagons, and Shand could hear their chatter and learned from what they were saying that the saloon was to be up and running in two days.

A tall, broad-shouldered man dressed in a grey frock-coat and wearing a curly-brimmed derby hat was walking around superintending the work. He had the look of a gambler about him, his tanned face sweating in the hot sun. He was dark-haired, and a black moustache curved over his thin-lipped mouth. He was moving around hurriedly, shouting orders and advice but doing nothing constructive, and the workers hurried to obey him.

That would be Simp Rawley, Shand decided, and wondered how best to get at the man. He did not want to brace Rawley in front of the workers – the odds against him were too great, but Rawley did not look like he was planning to go any place else in the near future. Shand curbed his impatience and waited stolidly, aware that he was too well-known to be able to reveal himself and confront Rawley.

He watched the scene before him for more than an hour before his patience became exhausted, then sneaked back to his horse and stole away unseen. Once clear he returned to end of track, his mind working on the problems besetting him. The obvious way to defeat Simp Rawley was by taking thirty men into the tent saloon when it opened for business and destroying it, but he was aware that Frank Merrick would not OK such a scheme.

When he rode into the construction camp he approached Hank Belmont and reported what he had seen at Kemp's Post. Belmont sighed heavily.

'How you gonna handle it, Cole?' he asked.

'That depends on Merrick,' Shand replied. 'I'm gonna have to toss it into his lap before I attempt anything. I'll send him a wire and wait here for his reply. If he ties my hands on this one then I'll be about ready to quit.'

'There must be easier ways of earning a living.' Belmont grinned. 'Rawley will be ready to open that business in a few days, and before then he'll pass the word into this camp of his existence. I won't be able to hold these men here when they learn of the saloon. There'll be a stream of them heading for Kemp's Post as soon as they finish work for the day, and we'll never get them back on the job. Hit Rawley hard, Cole, and put him out of business fast. What he's doing at Kemp's Post is more effective than any of the attacks we've suffered.'

'I'll get that wire off to Merrick.' Shand went on to the coach where the telegraph operator had an office.

The telegraph was connected to a post outside the coach which carried the message back along the wire to Longhorn Crossing. Merrick was not long in replying. Shand gazed at the terse message which gave him permission to smash Simp Rawley's saloon the instant it was opened for business, and enough men to do the job would be reporting at end of track within the next twenty-four hours. He sought out Belmont again and acquainted the camp boss with the news.

'There's no other way to handle it if we're to avoid losing our workers,' Belmont said. 'I didn't think Frank would let us down. You'll have to keep an eye on Kemp's Post, Cole. Don't let Rawley get close to opening for business. If our men got a whisper of drink and women being available, this place will look like an epidemic hit it.'

'I'll take care of it,' Shand promised. 'I'll get some supplies and lie up near the Post. Any men reporting here for me can wait around until I return.'

'I'll handle it.' Belmont nodded, and turned away when someone called him.

Shand went along to where the cooks were preparing the next meal for the 'rust-eaters'. He ate some hot food and obtained a sack of supplies, which he tied behind his cantle before riding out again, heading once more for Kemp's Post.

When he reached his vantage point in the gully he was surprised to see the progress Rawley's workers had made. The top of the canvas tent had been hauled up the posts that had been erected to support it, and already looked as if it could be used. Two of the canvas sides were rolled up to above a man's height and workers were hurrying in and out with items of equipment. A long, polished wooden bar was already being assembled inside, and the women were carrying in smaller items; tables and chairs, crates of glasses, bottles of liquor, gaming-tables, and the whole paraphernalia needed to operate the saloon.

Shand was impressed by the speed of the operation. Nothing had been left to chance, and he reckoned that at a pinch the business could be open for custom the very next day. Night was falling when he eased away from the scene. He rode a short distance into the shadows, a matter of two hundred yards, and made camp. He ate cold food before turning in, but his sleep was fitful, his thoughts too serious to permit rest.

About an hour before dawn he finally gave up any hope of sleeping and walked back to Kemp's Post, which was in darkness. A grey lightness appearing in the sky to the east hinted at approaching day, and he was able to make out details of the camp pitched by Rawley's crew. He sneaked in close to the big tent and crouched in the shadows. Presently a man armed with a rifle walked by almost within an arm's length without spotting him.

Silence pervaded the area. The night breeze was thrumming against the taut canvas. Shand walked around the perimeter of the tent until he reached the rear. In near darkness he scraped together a large pile of dried grass and heaped it against the canvas. Checking his surroundings, he satisfied himself that he was quite alone and produced a match, but, before he could strike it, a harsh voice called to him from behind.

'Get your hands up, mister. I got you covered.'

Shand tensed and lifted his hands instantly.

'You're kind of jumpy, ain't you?' he countered without turning around, hoping he could bluff his way out of this difficulty.

The muzzle of a rifle jabbed against his spine, and then a rough hand grasped his shoulder and spun him around. For a split second the rifle was not covering him, and Shand stepped in close and sledged his right fist against the man's chin. There

92

was a shocked cry and the man tried to bring his rifle into action but he was too close to Shand, who struck again, slamming his fist against the point of the man's chin.

Shand caught the guard as he fell and lowered him to the ground. He took a pistol from the man's gun belt and threw it and the rifle away into the surrounding darkness. He had lost his match in the tussle and produced another, striking it and shielding it against the breeze as he bent over the pile of dried grass.

The tiny flame of the match blazed up the instant it was thrust into the tinder-dry grass and he piled more on the quickly flaring conflagration. The canvas turned brown and then caught fire, and Shand moved back hurriedly.

He grasped the unconscious guard by the scruff of his neck and dragged him along as he headed away from the tent before pausing fifty yards away. He released his grip on the man, and when he turned to check the result of his effort at arson he was amazed to see some ten square yards of canvas burning furiously. Even as he watched the fire began to spread with astonishing rapidity, roaring greedily, its leaping flames devouring the whole side of the tent.

A rifle cracked sharply and echoes fled across the camp. Shand drew his pistol as he dropped to one knee, and when his prisoner began to move he struck a shrewd blow with his gun barrel and sent the man back to sleep. Another guard went running across Shand's front, shouting hoarsely to alert the camp. Shand arose and faded back into the darkness. He hurried to his horse, mounted, and rode away steadily. A shrewd glance over his shoulder showed him that the fire was blazing out of control, and he went back to end of track, elated by the knowledge of a job well done.

SEVEN

The sun had climbed to half-way between the horizon and its noon position by the time Shand reached end of track. The day's work had been in progress since first light and rails were being laid fast and efficiently. When Shand dismounted outside Belmont's coach the camp boss appeared on the top step.

'We had some trouble here at sun-up, Cole,' Belmont rapped. 'Shots were fired from outside the perimeter. Three men were killed at breakfast. I sent two of your troubleshooters, Tate and Ford, out to track the killers. They haven't returned, and I hope they've found a trail.'

'Where were the shots fired from?' Shand demanded, swinging back into his saddle.

'That stack of sleepers over there.' Belmont pointed out to the right. 'I saw two riders splitting the breeze after the shooting. They got clear before anyone here could get over their shock.'

Shand wheeled his mount and then paused to explain to Belmont what had happened at Kemp's Post. Belmont gasped, then shook his head doubtfully.

'You sure stuck your hand in a hornet's nest there, Cole. But it is what I would have done. Rawley can't operate with his equipment destroyed.'

'I'll take a crew with me when I go back there to finish off Rawley,' Shand said. 'Right now I'd better check out this raid.'

He set off in the direction indicated and passed the stack of sleepers, his intent gaze on the ground. There were plenty of tracks and he followed swiftly. It was in the back of his mind that Nat Poggin would pull a trick like murdering railroad workers in cold blood, and he knew he should have followed Poggin from town until he had run him down and killed him.

He rode at a gallop, following four sets of tracks. An hour later he crossed a ridge and reined in sharply. Two crumpled figures were lying on the ground ahead, and horror stabbed through him when he dismounted beside the bodies of his two troubleshooters, Tate and Ford. Both were dead, shot in the back, and the tracks gave mute testimony to what had happened. One of the two killers had dismounted and taken up an ambush position while the other rode on with his horse. Tate and Ford had passed the position and were shot in cold blood.

Shand saw where four sets of tracks went on, the killers leading the horses of the dead men. He swung back into his saddle and went on, grimly determined to run the killers into the ground. The tracks had been heading north but now swung ninety degrees in the general direction of Longhorn Crossing to the east, and Shand could tell that he was gaining hand over fist on his quarry. He was aware that an ambush could be awaiting him from any of the ridges he crossed, but sensed that the killers believed they were no longer being followed.

When he breasted a rise and saw a small ranch in the middle distance he reined about and got back out of sight in great haste. He dismounted, took a pair of field glasses from his saddle-bag, and bellied up to the crest into a position to observe the collection of small buildings. At first he thought the place was deserted. There was no stock in evidence. Then he spotted four horses tethered in scrub just to the right of the ranch house and recognized one of them as having been Jack Ford's mount.

Shand went back to his horse, climbed into the saddle and began circling the ranch. He went to left, staying out of sight of the buildings, and made his way to the rear. When he dismounted to take another look at the ranch he was well behind it, and could see a small corral at the back which contained six horses. He also spotted a guard walking around, carrying a rifle on his right shoulder.

He left his horse in cover, took his Winchester, eased his pistol in its holster and moved in carefully, getting down and crawling over the last yards until he slid into a depression and could lie watching the rear of the house. The guard had wandered around the building to check out the frontal approach, and Shand waited patiently to observe any life that existed out here at this desolate spot.

Twenty minutes passed before the guard reappeared around the left-hand corner of the house.

Shand was thirty yards out, and watched the man pass within feet of his position. The guard was looking around as he walked by slowly, obviously taking his duty seriously. He had barely disappeared again around the opposite corner when the back door of the house opened and three men emerged.

One man paused in the doorway, and Shand felt a pang of excitement stab through him when he recognized Nat Poggin. He drew his pistol, but stayed the movement as Poggin turned and went back into the house. Shand watched the other two men, who went to the corral. They saddled two horses and then rode out, heading east. One of the two looked familiar, and it took Shand some moments to put a name to him. Then he realized he was watching Bo Harmer, the boss troubleshooter for HTR; the man who took orders from Henry Padlow and ensured that the dirty work perpetrated against SWRR was carried out by hardcases like Poggin.

Shand estimated that at least eight men were in the house, including the two he had followed from end of track, so Poggin was safe for now – the odds were too great to tackle without help. He eased back to where he had left his horse in deeper cover, wanting to confront Harmer. Moments later he was following the two men, his right hand resting on the butt of his pistol as he pushed on to get within striking distance.

He drew his gun when he crossed a ridge and sighted Harmer and his sidekick just ahead. Both riders heard him at the same time and twisted in their saddles to look back. They reined in together and turned their horses, apparently thinking Shand had come from the ranch house and was one of their crew. When they realized their mistake both men reached for their holstered guns. Shand lifted his pistol and shot the man with Harmer. The blast of the gun hammered through the brooding silence and, as smoke flew from Shand's muzzle, the man pitched sideways out of his saddle.

Harmer was slower on the draw and sat with his gun only half-way clear of his holster. He did not move a muscle, aware that he would draw a slug if he did.

'Bo Harmer,' Shand said through his teeth. 'The boss skunk of HTR.'

'You got the advantage of me, mister,' Harmer replied.

'Get rid of your gun before we talk. Do it slow, with finger and thumb, and do it now.'

Harmer obeyed instantly and his pistol thudded on the ground. He was big and well-muscled, dark-haired, his tanned face sweating as he faced apparent death. He was in his mid-forties, and Shand had heard a great deal about his tough manner and brutal handling of his grim job.

'I'm Cole Shand,' he said. 'I expect you've heard of me.'

'Yeah, I know who you are. What are you doing out this way alone?'

'Trailing your killers. You've had a good day so far. Three construction camp workers murdered and two of my troubleshooters ambushed and killed. The two men who rode into that ranch back there just before you left were responsible, and I'll look them up later, but you can get down off your horse and we'll settle a few scores.'

'I won't draw against you,' Harmer said.

'You can please yourself about that.' Shand stepped down from his saddle, his gun steady in his hand, covering Harmer. 'Dismount,' he repeated.

Harmer got down and stood with his hands raised. He was sweating profusely, and kicked aside his discarded gun. Shand's eyes glinted.

'Pick it up,' he ordered,' and start using it whenever you like.'

'I won't fight you,' Harmer said. 'I'm not that stupid.'

'You'd prefer to shoot me in the back, huh?' Shand grinned. He waggled his gun. 'Go on and pick it up. You don't have a choice, Harmer. I'll count to three, and if you don't fight I'll shoot you.'

Harmer stood with his hands raised. Shand's finger began to put pressure on his trigger, but he knew he could not shoot a man in cold blood. He went forward to where Harmer was standing and the man backed away swiftly. Shand bent to pick up Harmer's gun. As he grasped the weapon a bullet crackled over his head. The crash of the shot came from behind, and he swung and dived to his left when he saw two riders bearing down upon him.

Both riders fired, their slugs kicking up dirt perilously close to Shand, who cut loose with his .45. The big weapon bucked in his hand and smoke flew. He hardly seemed to aim, but the nearer of the riders vacated his saddle and hit the ground hard.

Shand glanced around to check on Harmer and saw the man in the act of pulling a hide-out gun from a holster under his left armpit.

Shand threw a slug at Harmer as he triggered his gun. Harmer's slug creased the top of Shand's left shoulder as Shand's bullet took him in the chest. The surviving rider drew closer, still firing, and Shand returned his attention to the man as a slug plucked at his Stetson.

They fired together, and Shand felt the sting of lead in his left thigh. He dropped to one knee, lifting his pistol for another shot, but the rider had slumped in his saddle and the horse wheeled and went off at a gallop in a different direction. The rider fell to the ground before the horse had covered fifty yards. Shand heaved a long, bitter sigh as he tried to relax. His heart was beating fast, his pulses racing. The stink of gun-smoke was thick in his nostrils.

He went to Harmer first, bent over the man, and was relieved to find him alive. He wanted to talk to Harmer, but turned to the man who had ridden from the ranch with Harmer. He was dead, his face contorted, eyes half-open in a sightless gaze. Shand went to check the two riders who had come up and found both were dead. He returned to Harmer and checked the man's chest wound, shaking his head as he considered Harmer's chances of survival, certain the man would be dead before the sun went down.

Shand made Harmer as comfortable as possible, stanching the flow of blood from his chest and covering his upturned face with his Stetson. Harmer could not be moved, so Shand mounted and set out for town, intending to inform the doctor of the wounded man, although he expected it would be a waste of time. He rode fast to the east with a long way to go to Longhorn Crossing.

As he rode Shand considered what he had to do next. Poggin should be dealt with, and the business with Simp Rawley could not be delayed long. He was tempted to return to the ranch where he had seen Poggin, but common sense ruled and he continued, sighting the lights of town about an hour after sundown.

There was a light in Frank Merrick's office when Shand rode by, and he turned aside and dismounted wearily. Merrick was seated behind his desk, still working on a pile of paper work.

'Ah, Cole!' Merrick sighed with obvious relief and got up from the desk, grunting and stretching. 'I've been hoping you'd show up. What's going on out there? I haven't had a word from anyone since Hank Belmont wired me this morning with news of three men killed at breakfast. What the hell are your trouble-shooters doing? Can't they stop that kind of thing? Hell, it ain't that big an area to watch.'

'If you ain't happy with the way I'm doing the job then get someone else in,' Shand told him, and went on to describe the action that had taken place after he left end of track.

'Have you told Doc to get out there after Harmer?' Merrick demanded.

'I haven't been anywhere yet, except here. You tell Doc. I want to get something to eat, and then round up six men. I plan to be back at that ranch at first

102

light, and if Poggin is still there I'm gonna kill him. Then I need to get back to Kemp's Post to finish off what I started there.'

'Tell me about that,' Merrick invited.

'I burned down the tent saloon. I need to go back and run Rawley right off the range.'

'Just a minute.' Merrick held up a hand. 'You ain't the only one with news, Cole. I got a wire from head office this morning. TC Jeffery, the vice-president of SWRR, is on his way here to look over the situation at first hand. He's expected to arrive some time tomorrow. I want you to be here to meet him and explain why we have to resort to violence to get things done. And you better get yourself a bath and a change of clothes before he shows up.'

'Is he some kind of a lame brain?' Shand demanded. 'Anyone with half the sense of a wall-eyed bronc could see what's going on from the reports you send back East. I just told you what I've got to do, and I'm wasting time right now. I'll be riding out again within the hour, and I won't be back until Poggin is dead and Rawley is heading for other parts.'

'OK. But get back here as soon as you can,' Merrick said, shaking his head.

Shand departed to take his horse along to the livery barn. He tended it, then went to Doc Gilroy's house. The doctor came to the door in response to Shand's knock.

'Don't tell me you've shot someone else in the shoulder,' Gilroy said. 'I've just sat down at the table to eat.'

'You're lucky,' Shand told him. 'I've still got a lot to do before I can eat, and I wanta be riding out of town inside of an hour.'

He explained about the shooting near the derelict ranch. Gilroy protested furiously.

'I can't ride that long way tonight. I got Mrs Taylor in confinement, and all the signs are that the baby is due before dawn. You're talking about the old Carter place. Why didn't you bring him in?'

'The ride would have finished him off. I reckon he's dead even now, but you being a doctor, I thought you'd wanta ride out and do what you can, if you're not too late.'

'You reckoned he would die?' Gilroy asked. 'You've got knowledge of wounds, Cole. What are his chances?'

'I hit him in the centre of the chest, and I didn't think he would see the sun go down.' Shane turned away. 'But don't worry about him, Doc. He was trying to kill me so my conscience is clear.'

'So why come and tell me about him?'

'You're a doctor, ain't you?' Shand grinned and departed.

He went along the street to Abby Swain's restaurant, which was at its busiest. Abby was superintending her staff, and when Shand caught her eye she waved and signalled towards the back room. Shand entered to find Barbara standing in the kitchen doorway, and she smiled at him. She was evidently working, and looked quite fetching in a black dress and small white apron.

'Take a seat, Cole,' she said. 'I'll get a meal for you.

Abby has told me your likes and dislikes.'

'Thanks.' He sat down. 'I'm hungry enough to eat a horse, and I don't have much time to spare. I'll be riding out in an hour.' He got up again. 'Heck, I just remembered something important I gotta do. I'll be back in a few moments.'

He departed quickly and went back to Merrick's office. The area superintendent threw down his pen and leaned back in his seat when he saw Shand. He had an expression of deep worry on his rugged face.

'What is it now?' he demanded. 'I'll never get through this paper work.'

'Have we got any troubleshooters in town?' Shand asked. 'I need at least six men to back me when I go for Poggin.'

'I've already fixed that for you. They'll be waiting at the livery barn when you're ready to ride out. You'd better take my horse. I reckon that grey you've been forking the last two days is about all in.'

'Thanks, Frank. I ain't had a chance to get myself a mount since I came back. I'll take care of that detail when this business is done. I'm gonna eat now, and I'll be riding out soon after.'

He went back to the restaurant and sat down to a meal. Abby joined him, a cup of coffee in her hand, and she watched him eating for several moments. When he looked up and met her eyes she shook her head.

'I don't want to spoil your appetite, Cole,' she said gravely, 'but I think you should know that Simp Rawley is in town, and he's hopping mad about the way his tent was burned down. He wanted you arrested, and was furious when he couldn't find a law man. A guard told him you were seen crouching behind his tent over a heap of dried grass with a match in your hand.'

'I doubt that,' Shand replied. 'It was too dark. Where is Rawley at? I'll look him up. He's saved me the job of riding back to Kemp's Post.'

'He's booked into the hotel. He came to town to report to the law, and they haven't even appointed another marshal yet. Rawley sent a wire to the sheriff over in Blackwood, and he's gonna wait for a deputy to show up. You'd better be watching your back, Cole. Rawley has a gunnie in tow, and I heard him tell the man to get you any way he can.'

'Is that so?' Shand nodded. 'What does the gunnie look like?'

'He's tall and thin; wears a black store suit that's a size too big for him. He's got a pale face, badly pock-marked, and wears a fancy gun-rig studded with silver conchos. When I saw him I got a shiver down my backbone. His eyes are merciless.'

'I never heard of anyone being killed by a gunnie's appearance.' Shand laughed. 'I've been knee-deep in his kind ever since I took on this job, Abby, and I take them as they come. If one of them should get lucky, well, I've killed my share of them, and I've always accepted that one of them one day will be faster than me and put an end to my career.'

He saw a stricken look appear on Barbara's face.

'Don't worry about it,' he told her. 'Those two-bit gunnies never amount to much. Say, if you cooked this steak, Barbara, then Abby will have to look to her laurels. If you decided to set up your own eating-house in town, you'd kill off this place.'

'Don't go putting ideas into her head, Cole,' Abby reproved with mock gravity. 'I want Barbara to start taking some of the work-load off my shoulders. I'm beginning to feel the pace of running this business and Barbara has showed up at just the right time to take over.'

Shand got to his feet, towering over Barbara's slim figure. He looked down into her brown eyes, feeling that he could easily forget his strict attitude towards women in general and make an exception where she was concerned. He felt a need to get to know her, and did nothing to block his emotions, but he was aware that time was against him.

'I hope you don't think I come in here as a free-loader,' he said. 'Has Abby told you that Frank Merrick pays her weekly for what I pack away in here?'

'Yes.' Barbara nodded. 'I did ask if you got special treatment because of who you are, and she assures me that you're definitely not a free-loader.'

Shand grinned and departed, but his face sobered quickly after leaving the two women. He went out to the street and stood for a moment on the sidewalk, his back against the wall, his keen gaze probing the shadows surrounding him. His hand dropped to the butt of his holstered gun when a dark figure eased out of the shadows to his right.

'Hold it, Cole. This is Rio Walton. Merrick told me to wait for you at the livery barn with some of the men, but I heard there's trouble stalking you in town so I've been watching your back. Simp Rawley is in the hotel right now and his pet gunnie is in the Red Steer, making big talk about what he's gonna do when he sees you.'

'Rio!' Shand relaxed a little. 'How you doing, pal? I heard you took a slug in the leg the day I was shot. Are you healed up now?'

'I've got a limp I didn't have before, but the pain is about gone now. I got into town a short time ago, and heard you've made another start on HTR.'

'It's the same old story, Rio. HTR are attacking and we're fighting them off. I'm on my way to look up that gunnie of Rawley's right now. Then I'll set Rawley on the trail back to where he came from.'

'I'll back you,' Walton said. 'Let's go get them. I heard Rawley's gunnie is called Gat Bender.'

'I've heard of him.' Shand spoke through clenched teeth. 'Say, he's real fast!'

Shand drew a sharp breath as they went on along the sidewalk. Suddenly, everything seemed to be happening at once. He realized that there were things he should have done before heading into another showdown, but it was too late now for anything but the job in hand. He paused outside the batwings of the saloon and glanced inside.

He realized at once that something was wrong, and it took him a moment to note the silence that reigned inside. There was no movement, no hum of voices, and the piano-player, seated at his instrument, was motionless in his seat, his arms down at his sides instead of thumping the keys. The men at the bar were like statues, as if they had been frozen into immobility by a blue norther. The tender was leaning on the bar, both hands in plain view, his gaze fixed on the tall, black-clad man standing in a cleared space before him.

Shand's gaze slid around the room as if it had been greased, looking for other strangers who might be in cahoots with Bender. He saw only faces he knew. He pushed through the batwings and crossed the threshold into the saloon. All heads swivelled in his direction, and he felt the power of those eyes registering his arrival. The silence deepened, if that was possible, but Shand's gaze was upon the two-gun stranger standing at the bar holding a whiskey-glass in his left hand, his right hand hanging limply at his side as if it were useless.

'Gat Bender,' Shand said, and his voice crackled through the tension that gripped the big room. 'I hear you've been asking about me. You're running with Simp Rawley.'

'Sure. Rawley's dough is good.'

'I'm Cole Shand, and I'm in a hurry.' Shand stepped forward. 'Let's get to it.'

The cold-blooded invitation slapped the ears of the watching men like a wet cloth wielded by the bar tender. Nobody moved or breathed. Time seemed to cut off and the moment of confrontation stretched away into eternity as Shand waited for Bender's reaction. He was aware of nothing but the man standing before him. He looked into a pair of slate-grey eyes that were expressionless, impersonal, but would signal the start of the action a split second before any hostile movement began.

Bender erupted incredibly swiftly, his right hand moving in a blur of speed. Shand saw an almost imperceptible flicker in the gunnie's eyes and set his own hand into motion. The crash of two guns split the silence in a single blast of violence and gun-smoke flew. Shand stood motionless, as if rooted to the floor, and Bender jerked under the impact of a .45 slug striking his flesh. His right hand released its grip on his pistol, which thudded to the floor, and there was disbelief on his weathered features as he bent his left elbow and clawed out his second gun.

Shand fired again, rattling the row of bottles on the back shelf of the bar, and the bullet smashed into Bender's chest. The gunnie went over backwards and pitched to the floor, blood spurting from the half-inch hole that had been blasted through his heart. Echoes fled the scene and, as silence returned, the saloon came back to normal. Men drew breath again, and chatter broke out. Shand holstered his gun and turned abruptly to leave, followed by an awed Rio Walton. His thoughts were already concentrated on the problem of Simp Rawley.

EIGHT

Several townsmen were on the sidewalks, converging on the saloon, attracted by the shooting. Shand pushed through them and walked to the hotel with Walton at his side. He was tense inside, and offered up thanks for the speed that had enabled him to shade Bender's draw. He wondered how long he could go on before he met the gun that would prove to be faster, and shook his head, trying to rid himself of the grim thought. He made his way into the hotel and went through the lobby to the right to check the bar. As he suspected, Simp Rawley was inside, a whiskey-glass in his hand, apparently awaiting Bender's report on the shooting. It was obvious by Rawley's manner and expression that he thought he already knew the outcome of the action.

'Rawley, if you don't know me by sight then I'll introduce myself.' Shand paused beside the saloon-man. 'I'm Cole Shand. I run the troubleshooting section for SWRR. I heard tell that you've made some accusations against me concerning the fire at your tent out at Kemp's Post.'

Rawley set down his glass and looked up to meet

Shand's gaze. He glanced towards the door, and Shand laughed.

'If you're hoping for Gat Bender to show up and help you out of this then you'll have a long wait, mister. Bender tried what you paid him to do but wasn't fast enough. I expect the town will want you to pay for his funeral, seeing that you brought him into town.'

'You killed Bender?' Rawley spluttered over his words. His face paled and his hands began to tremble.

'Shot him dead centre. You sent a boy to do a man's job, mister. But he's yesterday's news now. Let's talk about you. Why do you think your tent was burned down? Did you believe you could get away with setting up near the railroad to disrupt our construction crew? It ain't the first time you've been burned out trying that trick. So who paid you to try again? I know who's back of it, but I'd like the name of the man you did a deal with. I suspect it was Henry Padlow. Can you confirm that?'

'I can set up a saloon anywhere I damn well please,' Rawley said in a low tone.

'Sure you can, but you can't open for business anywhere near railroad property, and you know that. So take heed. Pack up your wagons and pull out of Kemp's Post and you might save something from the mistake you made. I'll be riding out that way in a couple of days, and if you're still around I'll break you permanent. Have you got that? In fact, if I ever see your face again I'll rearrange it for you. That's all – short and sweet. Now get the hell out of town and stay out.'

112

Rawley almost choked as he tried to reply but his vocal chords were temporarily paralysed by shock. He stared at Shand for an interminable moment, fear showing plainly in his eyes, then he shook his head and hurried out of the bar. Shand glanced at Walton, who was grinning.

'Let's have a drink, Rio,' he said. 'Then you can watch friend Rawley until he pulls out. I'll be at the stable in thirty minutes and we'll ride out on another job that won't wait. We're gonna nail Nat Poggin.'

'It's about time that killer was laid to rest,' Walton agreed. 'I heard he was busted out of jail. Have you got any idea where he is?'

'I can lead you right to him,' Shand replied.

They had a beer, then Walton went out to the lobby. Shand was about to leave when Frank Merrick walked into the bar.

'I'm glad I've caught you,' Merrick said. 'TC Jeffery just got off the train from El Paso. He figured to catch us on the hop. I was bringing him here to get a room for the night but he saw the crowd at the saloon, and when he heard about Bender he wanted to take a look for himself. I left him in the saloon standing over that gunnie's body while I came for you. Come along and meet the man. He sure wants to talk to you.'

'I've got to ride out,' Shand said firmly. 'It ain't my place to meet him. What do you get paid for? Ain't it your job to jaw to the likes of him?'

'We got to sweeten him,' Merrick said. 'Don't make my job any harder than it has to be, Cole. If we can get Jeffery to see that there's no other way of handling the troubleshooting then he'll leave us alone in future.'

'OK. I can spare him ten minutes.' Shand turned to the door. 'Let's get it over with.'

They walked to the saloon, and had to shoulder their way through the crowd blocking the batwings. Gat Bender lay in a cleared space in the centre of the big room with the slight figure of Joe Ivey, the undertaker, standing over him. Shand's gaze went immediately to a tall man who was looking greatly out of place in eastern garb – an immaculate grey frock. coat and grey stovepipe hat.

'That's got to be Jeffery,' Shand remarked to Merrick, who had entered the saloon at his side.

'None other, and if you don't handle him right, Cole, we'll both be looking for new jobs before sun-up.'

Jeffery was asking questions of Ivey, who kept shaking his head. The vice-president of SWRR looked around, spotted Merrick, and came forward with a frown on his smooth face. He was tall and broad-shouldered, with large hands; one of them holding a silver-mounted cane. His blue eyes were narrowed, filled with tension, and told Shand much about the man. His lips were firm and pressed tightly together.

'Merrick, there's much I don't understand about this,' Jeffery said in a brisk, New York accent, his lips moving as if he was spitting out his words. 'Our man Shand was involved in a gun duel in this saloon. The undertaker tells me that Bender was waiting in here for Shand to arrive, and when he showed up they just exchanged a few words and then drew their guns and shot at each other.'

'That's the way it's done around here, Mr Jeffery,' Shand said.

'And who are you?' Jeffery's keen gaze swept over Shand from head to toe.

'Cole Shand. Chief troubleshooter for your railroad.'

'I've been impatient to meet you, Shand. Your name figures greatly in the reports I've been getting from Merrick. Tell me, why did you seek out Bender and kill him?'

'He drew wages to kill me on sight and I didn't want to take the chance that he might sneak up on me and plug me in the back, so I braced him.'

'Why didn't you inform the law and let them handle it?'

'I did.' Shand drew his gun and held it up. 'This is the only law in these parts, mister. The town marshal was shot a couple of days ago, and Doc Gilroy doesn't know yet if he will survive. The sheriff is some eighty miles from here, and might send over a deputy, but I wouldn't count on it. I think maybe you've got the wrong slant on what life is like out West. We do things differently, but we're usually right.'

'Tell me more,' Jeffery said.

'I'd like to but I don't have the time.' Shand smiled. 'There are two jobs I have to handle right away. One is a man named Nat Poggin, who was in jail awaiting trial for murder but was busted out a couple of nights ago, when a number of men were killed. I aim to put an end to his crooked life. He's killed a lot of our men. The other man is Simp Rawley, who planned to put up a tented saloon out at Kemp's Post and distract our men from the construction camp to drink and gamble instead of working, which would wreck our schedules. Rawley paid Bender to shoot me. I've seen Rawley and set him running, but I got to make sure he's gone and that he keeps going. I'll be out of town a couple of days, I expect, and if you can wait around for me to get back then I'll be pleased to fill you in on all the details of my job.'

'I'll do better than that,' Jeffery said instantly. 'I'm here to see exactly what lies behind the reports I've been getting, so I'll ride with you and watch you carrying out your duties.'

'I don't think so.' Shand grimaced as he shook his head doubtfully. 'I can't be responsible for your life, and I sure as hell won't try to do my job according to your rules. You got no idea what it's like out here, and you could be dead before you learn our ways.'

'I'll be responsible for myself.' Jeffery spoke in a tone that suggested he would have his way. 'And I'm not asking you to take me along; I'm ordering you.'

Shand looked into Jeffery's narrowed eyes, saw iron resolve in them, and smiled. Merrick, standing just behind Jeffery, was glaring at Shand and shaking his head warningly.

'You're the boss, they tell me,' Shand said. 'I have to be in position to confront some of the gang that's been giving us a lot of trouble, which means I'll be riding out in a few minutes on a trip of hard riding that will last till around sun-up. Can you ride a horse?'

116

'I learned to ride when I was a child in Vermont,' Jeffery replied.

'Riding around a paddock back East ain't the same as riding across the range.' Shand's tone was edged with impatience. 'Do you have suitable clothes? You can't ride in that get-up. And can you shoot? You would be expected to take care of yourself when the lead starts flying. I'm always short of men so we fight an uphill battle all the time.'

'I'm reckoned to be a fair shot with both rifle and pistol.' Jeffery smiled. 'We have a gun club back home, and I've hunted through the forest. I do know what it's all about.'

'And did the animals you hunted have guns to shoot back at you?' Shand persisted. 'Because out here they do. Nat Poggin is a big grizzly bear of a man who carries two pistols and has killed more than a dozen men. He's not to be reasoned with. You have to hope you're lucky enough to beat him to the draw and sharp enough to kill him before he gets you. He's not just a fair shot, Mr Jeffery. He can shoot the eyes out of a rat at twenty paces, and then some.'

'You paint a grim picture, Shand.' Jeffery smiled. 'But you won't shake my determination. I have to report to my board on my return to the East, so I'll ride with you, and you're wasting time trying to dissuade me.'

'OK.' Shand shrugged. 'Frank, get the boss into some suitable clothes and find a horse for him. I'm riding out shortly, and if he isn't ready when I am then I'll leave him behind.'

'I shall be ready,' said TC Jeffery.

Shand turned to leave, his mind already on what he had to do. He went back to the hotel and found Rio Walton standing in the foyer.

'Is Rawley still in the hotel?' Shand demanded.

'He ain't come down from his room yet,' Walton declared.

Shand felt a strand of impatience begin to unwind in his mind and suppressed a sigh. He glanced at the clerk standing behind the reception desk.

'Which room is Rawley in?' he asked.

'Second on the left at the top of the stairs,' the man replied. 'There better not be any trouble in the hotel.'

Shand mounted the stairs two at a time, followed closely by Walton. He rapped loudly on the door of Rawley's room. When there was no reply he stepped back a pace and raised his foot. The door flew inwards and Shand lunged into the room. He halted when he found it empty, and the half-open window indicated that Rawley might have departed by it. He raised the window and peered out at the balcony fronting the street.

A gun blasted from the shadows on the opposite side of the street. Shand saw the flash and ducked instinctively as shards of glass from the shattered window above his head tinkled around him.

Walton was already running from the room. Shand followed swiftly but by the time he reached the lobby he had given up all ideas of chasing the gunman. He grasped Walton's arm.

'Forget it, Rio. We're after bigger fish. Go down to the stable and saddle up Frank Merrick's horse for me, and pick out a cayuse for the big boss. He's riding with us, and I want you to keep an eye on him. Don't let him get into any kind of trouble, and don't let him see that you're watching out for him.'

'Riding with us ain't a job for any galoot just out from the East,' Walton observed.

'He's the boss. He pays our wages so what he says goes. Just keep him alive.'

'Sure thing, but he'll have to watch out for himself when slugs start flying.'

Shand went along the street to the store and bought some boxes of shells for his pistol and rifle. He gave the storeman a short list of supplies and waited until it was filled. He hefted a small gunny sack, and was leaving when Merrick appeared.

'Where's the boss?' Shand demanded. 'I'm about ready to leave. I'll have to travel fast if I'm to get in position out at the old Carter place by sun-up.'

'He's about ready to ride,' Merrick replied. 'He even brought along some riding-clothes in his baggage. You keep him alive out there, Cole.'

'Yeah, and I'll wipe his nose and tuck him in his blankets at night.' Shand grinned. 'He's got it in him to go right along with me, but that's what I would expect from a man who runs the railroad. It's his job to see how we work, and he'll sure have something to tell his folks if he lives to go back East.'

'Maybe I'd better ride with you,' Merrick mused. 'I could watch out for him.'

'You stay right where you are,' Shand told him. 'Someone's got to run this end of the business.'

'Good luck.' Merrick clapped a hand on Shand's

shoulder. 'I hope you get Poggin.'

'If I don't it won't be for the lack of trying.' Shand went along the sidewalk to the livery barn, carrying his supplies in his left hand while his right hand stayed close to the butt of his pistol.

Half a dozen men were waiting for him, their horses ready for travel. They were regular troubleshooters: men who could ride hard and shoot fast day or night. Rio Walton emerged from the barn as Shand reached it, leading two horses. Shand recognized Merrick's dun and grasped the reins. He tied his sack of supplies behind the cantle and put the boxes of shells in the saddle-bags.

'Where's Jeffery?' Shand demanded. 'Has he arrived yet? I told him I had to make haste.'

'I'm here,' Jeffery answered, and Shand turned to look critically at his boss, who emerged from the shadows along the sidewalk.

Jeffery looked uncomfortable in denims, a red-check shirt and riding-boots. He had exchanged his grey stovepipe hat for a flat-crowned Stetson. He smiled and paused for Shand's inspection.

'Will I need a gun?' he asked.

'You should have one for your own protection, not to do any fighting with,' Shand said. 'But when we get to where we're going I'll expect you to duck and keep your head down until the shooting is over.'

'You'll give the men we're after a chance to surrender, won't you?'

'Sure. We'll invite them to a dance here in town.' Shand smiled.

'More like a hanging party,' Walton cut in.

120

They mounted and set out with Shand leading. He watched Jeffery handling the horse he had been given, and was satisfied that his boss could ride well enough to go along. When they hit open range Shand set the pace at a mile-eating lope and night closed in around them. There was enough light from the star-studded sky to enable him to see where he was going. They rode in silence, the thud and beat of their hoofs on the sun-baked ground filling their ears with incessant noise.

Shand halted several times through the seemingly endless night to rest the horses, and Jeffery made no comment on what must have seemed to him like a punishing ride. It was just before dawn, with its greying sky and the faintest hint of crimson on the eastern horizon, when Shand finally called a halt.

'Stay quiet from here on in,' he warned. 'The old Carter place is about two hundred yards from here and I expect there'll be a guard out. We'll leave the horses here and walk in. Rio, take two of the men and cover the back of the place. There's a corral out there, and yesterday more than six horses were in it. The rest of us will go in from the front. Mr Jeffery, you stick close by me, and duck when the lead starts flying. I'll give Poggin and his sidekicks a chance to surrender before we go in shooting, although that'll be a waste of time.'

'You're running this operation,' Jeffery said. 'I'll follow you closely. Handle this in your usual manner.'

Shand smiled as they knee-hobbled their horses, took their rifles from saddle scabbards, and moved out silently. Shand walked briskly through dense

121

shadows that lightened imperceptibly with each passing moment, and when he halted again they could
see the faint outline of the Carter ranch house close
by. Walton went off silently with two of the men,
making for the back of the house, and Shand
motioned for the remaining pair to take up firing
positions.

'While I'm waiting for Rio to get into position I'll
move in and try to locate the guard. There's sure to
be one. If I can take him prisoner we might learn
who is in the house before we go in. Don't anybody
make a sound, and don't shoot me when I return.'

The sky was beginning to yield its even grey colour
to the orange fire of the sun spreading along the
eastern horizon. Shand would have preferred it to be
darker, but wasted no more time. He moved slowly,
easing through the shadows towards the house, his
keen gaze searching for sign of a guard. He slid into
the cover of a stunted tree and lay watching the yard,
appreciating the great silence that enveloped the
little ranch.

A horse stamped, the sound coming from the
rear of the building, and Shand waited stoically as
daylight strengthened. There were no other sounds
in the early morning, and he was about to circle the
house to check the number of horses in the corral
at the rear when a man carrying a rifle stepped
into view from around the left-hand corner of the
house.

The guard crossed the front of the house, seemingly ignoring his surroundings, and Shand sneaked
forward, Winchester in his left hand, his gaze fixed

on the guard's back. The man stepped out of sight around the corner of the house to continue his patrol and Shand ran forward silently, rounding the corner and colliding with the guard, who had stopped to light a cigarette.

'What the hell!' The guard was shocked by Shand's appearance, and tried to swing his rifle into action.

Shand drew his pistol and slammed the barrel against the side of the man's head. There was a dull thud as the cold metal made contact, and he reached out and grasped the man by the shoulders as he crumpled. He removed the guard's weapons, then peered around. There had been no sound. He hefted the man across his shoulders and started away from the house at an angle, not wishing to cross the open space in front of the building. He reached a depression some yards out from the corner and eased the unconscious man to the ground.

He checked the open space around him and saw Jeffery peering at him from the spot where he had been left. He wondered what the vice-president of SWRR was thinking at that moment. He cut his musing when the crackle of shots blasted through the silence. The disturbance occurred at the rear of the house; Shand looked towards Jeffery and signalled for one of the troubleshooters to be sent forward to take charge of the prisoner. He was chagrined to see Jeffery coming forward alone, clutching a rifle one of the others had handed him.

Jeffery arrived and dropped into the depression.

He was breathless, and gazed at the now stirring guard, apparently fascinated by the action that was evolving.

'You should have stayed out of it,' Shand said harshly. 'I wanted one of the others to come and watch this prisoner.'

'I can handle that chore,' Jeffery replied. 'What is that shooting about? I hope Walton didn't open fire first.'

'Walton wouldn't do that. I guess someone is trying to leave the house by the back door. Take this pistol and keep this man covered. You're too close to him in here for a rifle to be effective. Don't let him take your gun off you. I must look round the back.'

The shooting had slowed to an occasional shot, and Shand glanced around. He left Jeffery with the prisoner and ran along the side of the house to the rear corner. Gun smoke was drifting across the corral and the back of the house. He saw Walton crouching in the corral, pistol uplifted, and waved to attract the man's attention. Walton spotted him and waved an acknowledgement. Shand saw that there were only five horses in the corral.

He moved along the back wall of the house towards an opened window that overlooked the rear, from which someone in the house was firing into the corral. The muzzle of a rifle was showing at the window and he flattened himself against the wall beside the aperture when the weapon fired. Walton replied with two shots that splintered the woodwork almost beside Shand's head. The rifle inside was jerked back as the defender ducked, and Shand took advantage of the fact to reach the window and thrust his pistol inside.

A man he knew by sight as a rider for HTR was in the act of leaning forward with a Winchester at his shoulder, the muzzle pointing towards the corral.

'Throw the rifle outside,' Shand rapped, 'or I'll kill you.'

The man was at a disadvantage, aware that he could not bring his weapon to bear on Shand. He thrust the rifle forward and let it fall outside the window.

'How many of you are there in the house?' Shand asked.

'Two, and there's a guard outside.'

'We've got him. Get rid of your Colt and then call the other man in here.'

The man drew his pistol from its holster and tossed it on the floor. He half-turned and shouted a name. At that moment there were shouts from outside, at Shand's back. He whirled and crouched. A man was emerging from the back door, and levelling a pistol at him. At the same time he saw Jeffery at the far corner of the house. The railroad boss fired the pistol he was holding.

Shand dropped to one knee instinctively and heard a bullet crackle past his head. He thought it was Jeffery's slug that almost nailed him, but the man in the doorway took a short pace forward, his gun spilling from his hand, and then twisted and fell upon his face in the dirt. Shand jerked upright, lunged to the window, and was in time to see the man inside the room bend and scoop up the pistol he had been forced to drop. The next instant he was shooting at Shand from close quarters.

NINE

Shand clenched his teeth and triggered his pistol as the gunman fired. Gun-smoke flared, and he felt the pain of a slug creasing the top of his left shoulder. He squinted and peered through the drifting smoke, certain that he had hit his target, and saw the man in the room dropping to his knees. His brain seemed to cringe from the heavy detonations of the shooting and his ears were ringing. He turned as Rio Walton came running to his side.

'There are just three of them, Rio. One is a prisoner and the other two are down.' He glanced towards the back door, where Jeffery was standing over an inert figure. 'Did you or the boss shoot that man?'

'I was covering him from the moment he stepped into the doorway, but I held my fire to see what the boss would do. I didn't think he would shoot, but he did.'

'Get the two men out of the house and then check it out. My guess is that Noggin made tracks before we got here.'

'He'll sure run out of luck one day.' Walton turned

and signalled to the two men coming forward from the corral and led them into the house.

Shand gazed critically at Jeffery as he approached the man. Jeffery's face was pale and grim, but there was resolution in his eyes. He was holding a pistol in two hands, and heaved a long sigh when Shand halted before him.

'Thanks for saving my life,' Shand said. 'Just tell me one thing. Did you give him a chance to surrender before you shot him?'

'There was no time.' Jeffery shook his head. 'I came around the corner and saw him lifting his gun to shoot you; I fired instinctively.'

'That's the way it usually works.' Shand spoke softly. 'Maybe we'll have a different policy to guide us after this. I'm glad you came along, Mr Jeffery.'

'I said I wanted to see things for myself, and it has been an eye-opener. What happens now?'

'I'll question the prisoners. The man we came out to get is not here. And what about that prisoner I left you guarding?'

'When I heard the shooting out back I hit him with the barrel of my pistol and rendered him unconscious.' Jeffery smiled. 'I wanted to see what was going on. I hope nothing of what we are doing here is against the law.'

'I told you back in town: we carry the law in our guns. Let's get busy, shall we? I want to get on Nat Poggin's trail.'

They went around the side of the house to find their prisoner beginning to stir. Shand covered the man with his pistol.

'Where's Nat Poggin?' Shand demanded, dragging the prisoner to his feet and holding him steady with his left hand.

'Who's he?' the man countered, holding a hand to his head. He staggered, and Shand tightened his hold, his fingers twisted in the material of the man's shirt, keeping him on his feet with sheer brute strength.

'I saw him here yesterday,' Shand said grimly, 'just before I shot Bo Harmer.'

'You killed Harmer? That was the reason Poggin moved out. Our prowler guard found Harmer on the trail to town, and he was dying fast.'

'So where did Poggin head for?'

'He's gone to raise hell for SWRR, what else?'

Rio Walton approached. 'There's no one else in the house but the two wounded men,' he reported, his face showing disappointment. 'One of them is like to die any time; the other will need the doc, but he might not survive the ride back to town. There's no sign of Poggin.'

'He left here yesterday. Circle around the corral for tracks heading out and we'll follow him.'

'He could be anywhere right now,' Walton mused. 'He's got a big start on us.'

Shand went into the house with Jeffery following and checked through the rooms, finding nothing of importance. They went outside by the back door and saw Walton walking away from the corral, studying the ground intently.

'Rio is better than me at tracking, and I'm no slouch,' Shand said as he paused and looked around.

He turned his attention to Jeffery. 'I suggest you go back to town with the men I'm sending back with the prisoner,' he added. 'You surprised me, the way you kept up with us on the ride here, but you look like you're nearing the end of your rope, and we've got some more fast riding to do.'

Jeffery nodded. 'I won't argue with that, Shand. I need to get to the nearest telegraph and send some urgent messages. I'm happy with the way you're handling your job, and you have my full backing in anything you do. I'll try to make things easier for you by putting pressure on the men I know who run HTR. I may be able to get them to stop their attacks, but don't count on it.'

'Thanks.' Shand smiled. 'We've taken a beating lately because we have been restricted to fighting off raids instead of attacking. For a long time I've been planning to hit HTR hard. If I took some men to Devil's Gorge and smashed the span HRT have put across it we could halt them in their tracks for a long time. As it is, we are neck and neck with them, but with the trestle spanning Devil's Gorge destroyed they won't have a chance of beating us. After bringing down the gorge trestle, I'd work my way to their end of track, destroying everything on the way.'

'That sounds interesting. Go ahead and do it. I'll back you all the way, and when I return to the East I'll pull some strings and see if I can get some law protection for you. It's the only way to fight HTR. You've got the right ideas here on the spot, so keep at it, Shand.'

'Thanks.' Shand waved a hand to Walton and the

man came across. 'Send a man back to town with the prisoner and Mr Jeffery and I want someone to ride to our end of track with a message for Hank Belmont. We're gonna destroy HTR's trestle spanning Devil's Gorge, and I'll put that in writing and sign it. Meantime, we'll follow Poggin's tracks and put an end to his activities.'

'OK. I found tracks of four riders who left here around nightfall yesterday,' Walton reported. 'It looks like they headed towards our railtrack. I'll tell Mason to ride to end of track with your message.'

Shand nodded. He went into the house and wrote a message to Hank Belmont ordering him to send a demolition party to Devil's Gorge. He and Belmont had considered just such a move several times, and the construction camp boss was heavily in favour of it. When Mason rode out with the message, Shand heaved a great sigh and went to his horse. He rode out with Walton and three troubleshooters at his back. Tracks were plain on the ground but he was aware that too much time had been wasted. Poggin had a lead of many hours, and Shand hoped he could stop the hardcase before much more damage was inflicted on SWRR.

When Poggin's tracks cleared the ranch Shand was surprised to see that they veered east, as if heading for Longhorn Crossing, and he began to worry about Poggin's intentions. The killer could be on his way to exact vengeance on the town for his term of imprisonment there. He broached the subject with Rio Walton, and the troubleshooter nodded grimly.

'That thought has crossed my mind,' he admitted.

131

'I think you may be right. He's an evil cuss, and never forgets a slight or a bad turn. He may be heading for town to get the drop on you and anyone else he thinks has made life difficult for him. I think we'd better push on as fast as we can and see where these tracks lead to.'

They rode on and eventually reached the rail-tracks that linked Hank Belmont's construction camp with Longhorn Crossing just east of the spot where the trestle-bridge had been destroyed. The tracks continued alongside the track in the direction of the town, and Shand wondered what was in Nat Poggin's evil mind.

The afternoon was well past and the first shadows of evening were drawing into the sky when Shand spotted the buildings of Longhorn Crossing on the skyline. The interminable tracks of the four horses that had left the corral at the old Carter place were still in plain view. They had found the spot where Poggin had camped for the night, and as they rode towards the town Shand realized that he had been too far behind Poggin to put a stop to whatever the hardcase had contemplated.

Just outside of town they came across a spot where two of the four horses had halted while the other two went into the livery barn on the outskirts.

'I reckon Poggin stayed out,' Walton observed. 'He's too well known.'

'If he did then he rode in later,' Shand decided. 'Let's get on and find out what has happened.'

'Poggin might have come here for supplies,' Walton hedged.

Shand nodded and they continued to the stable. As he put his horse in a stall Walton uttered a cry, and Shand went to his pard to find him standing over the dead body of Mort Enderby, the stableman. Enderby's shirt front was saturated with blood. Shand dropped to one knee and examined the wound. When he looked up at Walton his eyes were filled with shock.

'Knifed through the heart,' he said tensely. 'It looks like he was killed some hours ago. Take care of the horses.' He got to his feet. 'I'll check out the town.'

'I'd better watch your back,' Walton said curtly.

They went out to the street and walked along the sidewalk. Shand looked around alertly and soon realized that the main street was practically deserted. There were no horses tethered at hitch racks along its length and no townsfolk on the sidewalks enjoying the cooling air of approaching evening. It might have been his imagination, but Shand thought he could sense an air of brooding lying over the town, and was fearful of what Poggin had done.

Shand reached the batwings of the Red Steer saloon and peered inside. Harper, the tender, was behind the bar, and there were several men present. Shand ran his eye over the men, looking for Poggin, but there was no sign of the hardcase, and no strangers were present. He entered and walked to the bar, his spurs jingling. Harper looked round, then came scurrying along the bar towards him, his expression showing that he had a lot on his mind.

'Cole, I sure am glad to see you!' Harper rapped.

'There's been hell to pay in town today. Nat Poggin rode in early with three hardcases and met four strangers in here who were waiting for him. They took over the town. Frank Merrick confronted Poggin with a shotgun and was shot in the chest. He's at the Doc's house and likely to die. Poggin bullied the whole town for hours, and then went into the restaurant for food. When he left he took Abby Swain's niece with him as a hostage.'

'The hell you say!' Shand turned on his heel and hastened to the batwings.

He hit the sidewalk fast and went along to Doc Gilroy's house with Walton following closely. Gilroy came to the door in answer, and shook his head sadly at the sight of Shand's stricken face.

'I'm sorry, Cole. Frank died two hours ago. I couldn't save him, although he put up a big fight to live.'

Shand stood motionless for some moments, fighting shock. He drew a deep breath, restrained it until his lungs protested, and then exhaled slowly.

'Thanks, Doc,' he said at length. 'I'll see you later.'

He turned away, almost reeling in shock. Frank Merrick was dead, killed by Nat Poggin. He tried to come to terms with the knowledge, and went resolutely along the street to the restaurant. There were diners inside, and Abby Swain was standing by the kitchen door watching her waitresses at work. Abby uttered a loud screech when she saw Shand, and came waddling towards him, her arms outstretched. He saw a large bruise on the left side of her fleshy face.

'Cole!' Abby cried. 'Where have you been? I

134

thought you'd never get back. Poggin was here with some hardcases and they played up hell in town.'

'I've heard about it,' Shand said curtly. 'Is it true he took Barbara with him when he left?'

'I tried to stop him but he knocked me down.' Abby fingered the bruise on her face. 'When I came back to my senses he had gone, taking Barbara with him. That poor girl! I can't bear to think what might be happening to her.'

'How long ago did Poggin ride out?' Shand demanded.

'About three hours; and there were seven hard-cases with him.'

'And which way did they ride?'

'They passed along the street right outside this door, and rode away north. It looked like they were in a hurry to get some place.'

'They're heading back to HTR territory, I guess,' Walton said. 'Eight sets of tracks should be easy to pick up. Want me to take a look, Cole?'

'Sure thing, Rio. We're gonna follow Poggin clear into hell, if we have to. And check if there are any of our men around town doing nothing. I'll need half-a-dozen men behind me if I'm to finish off Poggin and his bunch. We'd better eat before we leave. There's no telling how long we'll be on the trail.'

'I'll have food ready for you in twenty minutes,' Abby said. 'Please bring Barbara back, Cole.'

'Hell and high water won't stop me,' Shand rasped. 'I wanted to make killing or recapturing Poggin my priority but Frank was against it. Now I'll get him.'

He went out to the sidewalk and looked around.

Walton was already checking for tracks in the rutted street. The sound of approaching hoofs attracted Shand's attention. He looked around and saw Jeffery arriving with one troubleshooter and the prisoner they had collected at the old Carter place.

Jeffery looked utterly exhausted, and his taut features set into harsh lines when Shand told him what had happened in the town.

'The more I learn of the situation around here the better I can understand all the reports of violence I've been getting,' Jeffery said. 'There's no law here. Why aren't you wearing a deputy sheriff badge, Shand? You could do that job easily enough.'

'It would get in the way of my job with the railroad,' Shand replied grimly. 'I shall be riding out shortly. Walton is looking for Poggin's tracks. We'll run him down and put him out of it before we do anything else.'

'And the young woman?' Jeffery asked. 'Will Poggin harm her?'

Shand shrugged. 'He's capable of killing her in cold blood, but I'm hoping he's holding her as a hostage.'

Shand looked at the prisoner, who was sitting his horse dejectedly.

'Have you got any idea where Poggin is riding to?' he asked. 'Did he mention his plans before he left the Carter place yesterday?'

'Nope. He said he was getting back into the business, that's all. I don't hold with what he's done around here. None of this has to do with the railroad.'

Walton came back to where Shand was standing

and he was nodding.

'I got their tracks,' he said. 'Nine sets plain as your nose. We need to hit the trail, but fast. What else we got to do around here?'

'Just eat,' Shand replied, and turned back to the restaurant.

Thirty minutes later, six railroad troubleshooters rode out of town with Shand leading them. They followed tracks that led to the north, and discovered that a mile out of town Poggin's party had been joined by another six riders, making fifteen all together. Shand raked his memory to review what lay in the direction Poggin was heading. The line HTR was putting through to Indian Pass lay more than seventy miles ahead, converging on the track SWRR was putting down, and it seemed to Shand that Poggin was on his way to report to his superiors in the town of Clear Water before resuming his savage attacks against their competitors.

They rode fast, hoping to catch Poggin quickly, but night was falling, and Shand tried to keep his thoughts from the plight that Barbara was in. When the shadows were almost too dense for them to see tracks clearly, Walton reined in and looked at Shand.

'Hey,' Walton rapped. 'Five riders turned off here and rode south-west.'

Shand reined in and dismounted stiffly. He dropped to one knee to examine the tracks, and confirmed what the sharp-eyed Walton had seen. Five of the riders had turned off. Shand stared into the growing darkness, wondering what lay to the south-west.

'I think those five are heading for the Carter ranch,' Walton mused. 'Do you reckon Poggin has taken the girl back to that run-down place?'

'What do you think, Rio?' Shand countered. 'I reckon the Carter spread is about thirty miles in that direction. We can't follow these tracks until sun-up, so I'll ride to the ranch and check it out. I'd better take a man with me. You follow these tracks in the morning, which look like they're heading to Clear Water, and I'll come back to this spot after checking out the ranch and follow you from here. That way we won't waste a lot of time. We need to get all of the men who were with Poggin today, so keep following the tracks until you catch sight of those killers.'

Walton shook his head. 'I should ride with you,' he said doggedly. 'If Poggin has gone back to that ranch then you'll need me to help you nail him.'

'You're the best tracker we've got,' Shand decided, 'so stick with these prints and run them down in the morning. If Poggin is still with his main bunch I want you to follow him until I catch up again. Don't try to take him. I wanta be on hand for that showdown. It's personal now between Poggin and me.'

'You're the boss,' Walton said. 'I'll do what you say, although I don't like it. Take Fallon with you. He's sharp with a pistol.'

Shand rode out with Burt Fallon at his side and travelled as fast as he dared, given the conditions surrounding them. He had covered this stretch of the range before and knew the ground fairly well. Darkness shrouded them until the moon showed later, and it was after midnight when Shand finally reined in and sat his tiring mount, looking around for shadowy landmarks that could pinpoint his position.

'I think we've come far enough to sight the Carter place,' he told Fallon. 'But it could be to the right or left of us. Why don't you get down and try to get some sleep while I take a look around?'

'No,' Fallon replied. 'If Poggin's got that girl then we better nail him quick. I wouldn't trust Poggin with a dog.'

'OK, you make a circle off to the right and I'll do the same in the opposite direction.' Shand tugged on his reins and turned his mount. His eyes were narrowed as he peered around. All he wanted was the chance of one shot at Poggin. He rode slowly, aware that Poggin would have been expecting some of his men to be at the ranch, and wondered at the killer's reaction to finding the place deserted.

He topped a rise and reined in to look around. Hope flared inside him when he saw a faint yellow light in the distance. He looked back for signs of Fallon, but he was completely alone in the darkness. He went on slowly, determined to force a showdown with Poggin.

When he drew nearer to the light the faint outline of the Carter ranch house took shape, and Shand was pleased with the way he had ridden almost straight to it. He dismounted, trailed his reins, then drew his pistol and checked its loads. He removed his spurs and went forward on foot, taking his time in the shadows, aware that he needed an edge to succeed against Poggin.

The light in the window of the ranch house attracted Shand like a magnet exerting influence on a horseshoe. He moved to the right of the house, not directly towards it, and eventually reached the right-hand corner of the building. There was enough starlight to enable him to see details close to hand, and he eased along the side of the house to the rear. When he could see the corral out back he spotted the shadowy figures of several horses in it, some moving restlessly; then he caught a glimpse of a slight movement to one side of the stockade.

Shand froze, his eyes narrowing as he tried to pierce the gloom. He eventually made out the figure of a man leaning against the horizontal poles of the corral, and then saw the tiny red glow of a cigarette as the man smoked. Shand did not move, and tense moments passed while the guard rested. It was five minutes more before there was any movement, and then the man walked away from the corral and headed straight for the corner where Shand was standing. He was only a few yards from Shand when a voice called from the back doorway of the house. Shand stayed his movement to attack and remained hidden.

'Hey, Donaghy, where are you? Nat said we got to reach that busted trestle on the SWRR line just before sun-up. Saddle our nags while I make some coffee, and then we'll get moving. We'll kill some more of those rust-eaters before breakfast.'

'Where is Poggin?' Donaghy demanded. 'Ain't he supposed to ride with us?'

'We do what he says, not question his movements,'

140

came the sharp reply, and Donaghy muttered softly as he turned around and went back to the corral.

Shand moved forward swiftly, swinging his pistol, and slammed the barrel against Donaghy's head. There was a low moan as Donaghy crumpled to the ground, and Shand struck again before grasping the hapless guard by the scruff of the neck and dragging him into the shadows around the corral. One of the horses became restless and whickered. Shand quickly disarmed Donaghy and then turned back to the ranch house.

He walked into the kitchen with his pistol ready, and covered the man making coffee, who half-turned towards him, grinning until he realized that Shand was not Donaghy. His smile faded and was replaced by shock. He started his right hand towards his holster but thought better of it and raised both hands.

'You're Cole Shand,' he said.

'That's right.' Shand disarmed the man. 'So you know who I am. And you must know why I'm here. Who else is in the house?'

'Poggin ain't, and that's a fact. He brought the girl and a few of us from our main bunch at nightfall, but left and cut off back to Longhorn Crossing a couple of hours before we reached here. He said something about grabbing some money from the girl's family. He's coming back here later.'

'Is the girl here?' Shand demanded.

'Sure. She's in the big room up front.'

'Take me to her, and play it straight or I'll bury you in the morning,' Shand ordered.

141

The man shrugged, crossed to an inner doorway and nudged it open. The door creaked slightly. Shand followed on tiptoe along a short passage to the big room at the front of the house where he had first seen the light at the window. The door to the room was invitingly ajar, and Shand restrained his breathing as his prisoner pushed it open and walked boldly into the room.

Shand followed closely, his pistol cocked. He placed his left hand on the man's shoulder as they crossed the threshold of the room, ready to thrust him out of the line of fire at his first sign of resistance. He caught a glimpse of Barbara seated in a chair across the room. A big man was sitting at a table, eating ravenously.

The man at the table was looking towards the door as Shand and his prisoner entered, and the next instant all hell broke loose.

TEN

The man reared up from the table, overturning the chair in his haste, his big right hand flashing to the butt of his holstered gun. Shand thrust his prisoner to one side and levelled his pistol, his eyes mere slits in the lamplight, his pulses racing. He saw the man's gun flip out from its holster and lift to line up on him. He triggered his Colt, felt the butt kick against the heel of his hand, then the room was filled with the flash and thunder of gun racket.

Shand's bullet smacked into the centre of the man's barrel chest. The man's trigger finger jerked convulsively and his weapon blasted, sending a slug into the top of the table. The impact of Shand's striking bullet knocked him backwards and he fell against the wall behind him, his feet becoming entangled with the overturned chair while he used his fast-draining strength in an attempt to get an aimed shot off at Shand, using two hands on his gun even as he pitched to the floor.

Again Shand's gun hammered, rocking the interior of the house with an echoing blast, and a red splotch appeared in the centre of the man's forehead. Shand turned quickly to check on his prisoner, and saw him crouching on the floor, his face expressing shock.

Shand exhaled deeply, ridding his lungs of the stink of gun-smoke. He motioned for the prisoner to get up, and at that moment a voice called from the front of the house.

'Shand, this is Fallon. Do you need any help in there?'

'Come in. It's all over here,' Shand replied.

Fallon entered, gun in hand, and whooped with pleasure when he saw the dead man sprawled against the back wall. Shand sent him out back to fetch in Donaghy from the corral, and then turned his attention to Barbara Madden. The girl was motionless in her seat, her eyes wide, her pallid face showing great shock. He drew a long breath of relief as he went to her.

'It's all right now,' he said, smiling grimly. 'You'll be on your way back to town shortly. Are you OK? Did Poggin harm you?'

Barbara shook her head, and made an effort to control her shock. Her hands were trembling. She attempted to stand, but fell back into the chair as if her legs were powerless. Shand went to her side, put a hand under her elbow and raised her, holding her steady.

'I wasn't harmed,' she said in a low tone, and suppressed a shudder. 'Poggin left us in the night. He said I would go back to Abby unharmed if he was paid two thousand dollars, and I think he rode back to town to get the money.'

'He would have killed you the minute after he received money,' Shand said. 'I guess we can stay here until sun-up, and then we'll take you back to town. So Poggin left you, and I was hoping to catch up with him here. I don't think I'll find him in town when we get there.'

Fallon returned with Donaghy, who was unsteady on his feet. The two prisoners sat together on the floor until Fallon found some rope and bound them. Barbara went into the kitchen to prepare food, and they were eating a meal as the sun showed in the sky. They were still eating when hoofs sounded in the front yard. Shand ran to the door, lifting his gun as he did so.

Four riders were coming across the yard, and relief filled Shand when he recognized Rio Walton leading them. He went out to the porch, holstering his pistol as he did so.

'I thought you were going to follow Poggin's men at dawn,' Shand said. 'What changed the plan?'

'After we made camp last night one of the men spotted a camp-fire in the distance. Poggin's boys had settled down for the night. I scouted around, saw Poggin, the girl and some of the men were missing from the camp, and decided to take the rest of them. They didn't put up much of a fight. We caught 'em flat-footed and shot the hell out of them. That left us free to ride after you, and here we are. How did you make out here?'

'You've missed the action.' Shand was filled with impatience. 'Poggin wasn't here but we've got the girl back. We're heading to town shortly. Give your

145

mounts a rest and grab some breakfast. I reckon we'll be making a big raid on HTR's construction camp and track after I've settled with Poggin.'

'That won't be before time,' Walton said. 'We've all talked of nothing else for weeks.'

Shand nodded. 'Mason will have given my message to Hank Belmont by now, and I reckon most of the men at the construction camp will be on their way to Devil's Gorge by noon tomorrow. We'd better get back to town, sort out any problems there, then ride for Devil's Gorge. If we blow that trestle then HTR will be finished. We'll be laying tracks through Indian Pass before they can clear away the rubble.'

Thirty minutes later they rode out for town. Shand was pleased with the way the situation was turning in his favour. At last he could contemplate the tactic he had struck upon months before but for which he had found no support. Now he would see the Devil's Gorge trestle go up in smoke. He sensed it was the master stroke that was needed to end this trouble.

It was the middle of the afternoon when they sighted Longhorn Crossing. Shand was practically exhausted after the many hours of pounding a jolting saddle. But he could not afford to think of resting, and his teeth were clenched with the effort of continuing as they rode in along the street. Walton turned in at the livery barn to put away his horse, but Shand expected to be riding out again immediately. He reined in at the hitching-rack in front of the restaurant and dismounted stiffly, his eyes searching his surroundings as he stretched to get the kinks out of his cramped body.

At his side, Barbara slid out of her saddle, and staggered as she stepped on to the sidewalk. Shand reached out a steadying hand and she smiled at him.

'You look as if you're ready for a long rest,' he said softly. 'Let's find out if Poggin came back here, huh?' He glanced at the troubleshooters who had been riding with them. 'Take those two prisoners along to the jail and lock them in a cell,' he told two of them. 'The rest of you get some food and a beer and be ready to ride out again as soon as possible.'

The men departed and Shand led Barbara into the restaurant. There were no diners at this time of the afternoon, but Abby was in the kitchen, cleaning pots and pans. When she saw them she dropped a skillet and came hurrying to embrace Barbara, then threw her arms around Shand's neck. He tried to fend her off but she would not be denied.

'I knew you'd bring Barbara back,' Abby gushed. 'Poggin showed up here this morning, asking for money, and I gave him two thousand dollars for Barbara's safe return.'

'I'll get the money back when I see him,' Shand said quietly. 'Has he left town?'

'He didn't stay at all. I got the money from the bank and he rode out in the same direction he took yesterday when he forced Barbara to go with him. I watched him out of sight, and he was pushing along at a fast clip.'

'Then I can't stay.' Shand looked at Barbara. 'I don't think you'll have any more trouble from Poggin, but be careful until I get back. No one is safe with Poggin on the loose.'

147

He left the restaurant, saw Walton coming along the sidewalk, and waited for the man to reach him.

'Poggin was here this morning,' Shand said. 'He collected two thousand dollars from Abby Swain and pulled out fast. 'I'm gonna check the railroad office for the latest news, and then we'll ride out after Poggin. This time I hope to catch him. Get some food, Rio, and see that the others stock up. Ask one man to stay at the law office, if they haven't taken on another marshal yet, and we'll sort out that situation when we get back.'

He went on to the railroad depot. A pang of emotion stabbed him deeply when he entered the office to find TC Jeffery seated at the desk instead of Frank Merrick's familiar figure. He reported Poggin's activities in the town and Jeffery shook his head.

'Poggin seems to bear a charmed life. But keep right on after him, Shand. I've received a wire from Hank Belmont at end of track saying that Mason arrived there with your message for a demolition gang to hit HTR's trestle spanning Devil's Gorge, and a large party of our construction workers is getting ready to set off. Can you ride over to the gorge in time to supervise the job?'

'I'm leaving immediately,' Shand said. 'I'm gonna try and ride down Poggin; he's heading in the right direction for me, but I'll leave his trail if I have to. I want to be on hand when that trestle is blown.'

'Is there anything I can do to help?' Jeffery asked. 'I have a feeling that, as your superior, I ought to ride with you.'

Shand shook his head. 'It would be better if you took care of this end of the operation,' he said.

Jeffery nodded and Shand departed. He paused in the street and checked his surroundings. He needed to get some food and started towards the restaurant, but hoof-beats alerted him and he swung around to see three men riding along the street in his direction. He narrowed his eyes to pick out their details against the slanting rays of the sun, and shock jolted through him. The foremost of the trio was Simp Rawley.

The saloonman shouted and spurred his horse, followed by his two companions. Shand drew his pistol and dropped to one knee as the three riders began to shoot at him. Quick gun-blasts shattered the deep silence and gun-smoke flew. Shand triggered his Colt, fighting his weariness as he traded lead with the trio.

Rawley took a bullet in the chest, slipped sideways and fell from his horse to thump into the dust of the street. Shand felt a bullet tug at the holster on his right hip but continued shooting, his lips drawn back from his teeth in a snarl of defiance. Sweat began to run down his forehead. Another gun joined in the action from along the street and the remaining two riders were swept from their saddles in a hail of concerted lead.

Shand got to his feet. Rio Walton was running towards him, a smoking gun in hand, and Shand heaved a long, shuddering sigh as he went forward to look at his attackers. Walton paused beside the fallen Rawley, then came on, grinning. Shand found the other two gunmen dead. He waited for Walton to reach him.

'Rawley figured he had some unfinished business with you, Cole,' Walton observed. 'I spotted him coming along the street just as the shooting started. Looks like we're tidying up the loose ends, huh? We shoulda killed Rawley in the hotel and let the chance go by, but he's dead now.'

'We're getting through the opposition,' Shand replied. 'Let's get something to eat and then set out after Poggin. He'll have to be our second chore unless we can come up with him real quick. We need to be at Devil's Gorge as soon as we can make it. Belmont and a demolition team will be there come morning.'

They ate a quick meal which Abby happily prepared for them, then they departed for the stable. Shand borrowed the town marshal's horse again, and four of them left town at a fast clip, heading north. They rode for Devil's Gorge, and Shand could only hope that he would come up with Poggin on the way.

Night came while they were riding steadily towards HTR's track and Shand had no intention of stopping. He knew the area very well, and fought against tiredness as he maintained the mile-eating pace. He pushed all thoughts of Poggin into the background of his mind, aware that smashing HTR's chance of victory in the race to Indian Pass needed every ounce of his concentration. They rode through the night, making occasional halts to rest their horses.

When daylight came Shand looked around to get his bearings. Judging by the landmarks he realized that he was some five miles from Devil's Gorge. He grinned tiredly at Walton.

'That's what I call good riding,' Walton observed. 'We rode through the night and hit the spot right on the nail. The HTR track is a couple of miles ahead. I've been this way before.'

Shand nodded. 'Let's get on and see if Belmont and his men are at the gorge,' he said.

They rode on, angling to reach the railroad track that would lead them to Devil's Gorge. Shand kept a watch on his surroundings, hoping to catch a glimpse of Nat Poggin but knowing he could not be so lucky. The wilderness seemed devoid of human life other than their own, and he fought down his disappointment. He wanted Poggin alive. It would give him great pleasure to see the killer back in jail and to watch his subsequent execution.

They came in sight of the gleaming rails of HTR's track leading to their end of track and the distant Indian Pass, and angled left towards the ridge in the distance where a trestle bridge spanned the Devil's Gorge. They traversed rising ground, following the track through a cutting that led to the gorge. Presently Hank Belmont and another guard arose from cover and stood with rifles aimed at them.

'I was beginning to think you wouldn't get here in time for the big bang, Cole,' Belmont greeted with a grin. 'What took you so long? I expected you to take care of the guards before I arrived, and found we had to do your work for you. We got five prisoners who were guarding the trestle. They say there's a work train due shortly, and we'll be ready to blow the tres-

151

tle as the train crosses it.'

'I think you should blow it the minute you're ready to,' Shand said instantly. 'Bring that trestle down and it'll finish HTR, which is what this is all about.'

'OK.' Belmont looked crestfallen.

'Have you got guards out to watch for troubleshooters patrolling the line?' Shand asked.

'Only in the direction of their end of track. I'm covering this side.'

'You should be on the trestle, supervising the preparations for demolition,' Shand said firmly. 'We'll take over this side while you do what you came for. Give us a signal when you're ready to light your fuses and we'll get clear.'

'Sure thing.' Belmont nodded. 'We're well ahead with the job.'

Shand dismounted and trailed his reins. He walked along the track to the brink of the gorge and peered into the chasm, which was some 150 feet wide, 170 feet deep, and spanned by a massive wooden trestle-bridge. He looked down and saw a dozen men climbing around the woodwork, placing explosive charges in strategic places and stringing out fuse-wire.

'It's looking good,' he commented. 'Get it done, Hank. The sooner the better.'

Belmont nodded and moved on. Shand retraced his steps to where their horses were waiting. Walton was stretched out on the ground, resting.

'Let's move back at least half a mile,' Shand instructed. 'There'll be one helluva bang when that trestle goes, and it will come down in bits over a wide area. We'll need to get under cover.'

They rode back along the track until they were clear of the ridge, then dismounted. Shand tried to relax, but anticipation gripped him. They settled down in a depression, but as soon as he touched the ground Shand found his eyelids closing. Sleep tried to claim his senses and he got quickly to his feet.

'I'm gonna take a ride, Rio,' he declared. 'If I don't do something I shall fall asleep. The rest of you better keep awake.'

Walton grinned. Shand got up, swung into his saddle and urged his horse to walk alongside the track away from the Devil's Gorge in the direction the work train would appear. He was on a downgrade which ran for three miles before levelling out. The sun was hot on his back and lulled his senses. He tried to work out how many hours he had been without sleep but failed; too much had happened since his return to duty.

He rode to the top of a knoll one hundred yards on from where Walton and the others were waiting and reined in to look along the length of the track into the shimmering distance. A faint wisp of black smoke was staining the sky to the east. He reached for his field glasses and focused them. For some moments he watched the locomotive which was coming, pulling a dozen flat- and box-cars. It was still miles away, and he hoped Belmont would blow the trestle before the train reached the gorge.

The approaching train seemed to get no nearer as the minutes passed, and Shand sat slumped in his saddle as he waited. He used his glasses to inspect the surrounding rangeland, still hoping to spot Poggin.

When he returned his gaze to the train he was surprised to see that it had drawn much closer, travelling fast with thick black smoke belching furiously from its funnel – the fireman was shovelling coal into the firebox to raise sufficient steam for the long haul up the three-mile gradient leading to the trestle.

A movement along the track caught Shand's gaze and he lifted his glasses to see three riders emerging from a draw between his position and the nearing train. When he brought the face of the foremost rider into focus his teeth clicked together and his heart seemed to miss a beat. He was gazing at the vicious countenance of Nat Poggin. The killer rode close to the track and waved an arm to stop the train. Shand waited until he could see the locomotive slowing, then put away his glasses and drew his rifle.

He rode forward at a canter, closing the distance on Poggin as the train ground to a halt. Poggin spoke to the engineer, and then led his two sidekicks along the train to put their horses aboard a flatcar. Poggin heard the sound of Shand's horse approaching and swung around, reaching for his pistol as he did so. Shand reined in and lifted his rifle into the aim. He fired quickly to throw Poggin off his aim, and then triggered the rifle, sending a stream of slugs at the mounted trio. Bullets came in return and he dived from his saddle and hunted cover.

The train began to roll forward again. The engineer pushed a lever and released a cloud of steam from the engine, which shrouded the space between

Shand and Poggin. By the time the steam had dissi-
pated Poggin was no longer in sight. One of the
riders was lying beside the track and the horses were
galloping away.

Poggin and his sidekick had boarded the train.
Shand ducked as the fireman leaned out of the cab
with a rifle in his hands, then he fired. The fireman
pitched out of the cab and fell in a heap beside the
track. A pistol began firing at Shand from an open
doorway on a boxcar further along the train. He
lunged across the track and waited for the engine to
reach him. He saw the engineer's head and fired a
shot to make him duck. As the engine passed Shand
began running in the same direction and sprang on
to the steps leading up to the footplate.

He covered the engineer, who lifted his hands in
token of surrender, then returned to his job of
driving the locomotive. Shand looked around for
weapons, saw none, and began to climb over the
coals to get to the nearest flatcar. A pistol blasted as
soon as he showed himself; he returned fire, then
lunged forward to get clear of the tender. He
sprawled on to the flatcar, lost his balance and
grabbed at the nearest crate as he started sliding off
the train. A bullet splintered the crate only an inch
from his hand and he rolled desperately to get clear.

Bullets thudded into the crates, following his
movement across the flatcar. Shand came up into the
aim, paused, and snapped a shot at a man lying on
the crates towards the far end of the car. The man
dropped his pistol and fell off the train. Shand
pushed himself to his feet and ran over the crates,

wanting to get to the cover of the red-painted boxcar that was next in line.

Shand had a glimpse of Rio Walton and the rest of his men standing beside the track at the spot where they had been resting. He shouted for them not to get aboard but his words were shredded by the wind and he waved his hand to discourage them as he continued, gaining the roof of the boxcar and crawling over it.

Several bullets splintered upwards from inside the car. Shand dived to one side and fell heavily, blood spurting from his left forearm. He dropped flat and grabbed at a ventilator in the roof. More shots hammered and he sprang up and jumped down to the flatcar next in line. He landed awkwardly on some equipment that was covered with tarpaulin sheets and dropped his gun. Poggin appeared on the top of a boxcar well back on the train and started shooting as Shand scrabbled desperately for his gun.

Poggin got off one shot before his hammer struck an empty cartridge. He ducked out of sight to reload. Shand located his gun and snatched it up. The train was labouring up the steep gradient, the click, click of its wheels slowing with each passing second. Then the sound turned to a dull hollow roar. Shand glanced sideways and saw that the engine had passed the gradient and was now running on the trestle, gathering speed with each passing second.

Shand swung to one side and looked out to see nothing but empty space around the train. They were crossing Devil's Gorge. Horror struck through him as realization came. Belmont hoped to blow the trestle while the train was on it. He looked down for signs of the demolition party but saw no one.

A bullet struck a metal object under the tarp on which Shand was standing. He ducked and lifted his pistol. Poggin was shooting from back along the train. Gun-smoke drifted around the killer as he triggered his gun. Shand dropped flat and sent two quick shots in return, clipping the edge of a boxcar roof, and Poggin ducked.

Shand looked around again. The train was half-way across the trestle. He began to hope that Belmont had decided to let the train pass. He reloaded his pistol and watched for Poggin, ready to resume the fight.

Poggin suddenly appeared on the ladder on the side of the boxcar, and Shand caught the man's movement. He fired instantly and scored a hit. Poggin lost his gun and his feet slipped off the iron ladder. He hung by one hand, his feet scrabbling for a foothold. Shand held his fire, watching, and at that moment the most tremendous explosion he had ever heard shattered the silence and a great cloud of smoke and debris rose in the air behind the train.

Shand sensed rather than heard the wheels of the train change note again as he reeled sideways in shock, his ears deafened by the explosion. He saw Poggin lose his grip on the ladder and pitch backwards to disappear into space as the boxcar swayed in the blast. Poggin's body fell into Devil's Gorge, and a moment later the train was clear of the gorge, braking hard. Shand ducked as debris began to rain down – lengths of steel track and shattered pieces of the trestle – and then something solid caught him on the head and he pitched forward on to his face as a wave of darkness swept down upon him.

He came to in utter silence, and at first thought that he was dead. But Rio Walton and Hank Belmont were bending over him, concern showing on their shocked faces, and he looked around to find himself lying on the ground beside the train. His ears were ringing from the effects of the massive explosion. His head was hurting and there was blood on the front of his shirt.

'What in hell were you doing on the train?' Belmont demanded. 'I got the shock of my life when I saw you as I was about to press the plunger. It was touch and go, and only the front half of the train made it across the gorge.'

'Poggin got on the train,' Shand said dully. 'He fell off in the explosion and went down into the gorge. I've got to get down to him. He's got Abby's two thousand dollars on him.'

He tried to rise but slumped back, shaking his head.

'I'll go down,' said Walton. 'You take it easy, Cole.'

Shand nodded. He felt strangely lethargic. Nothing seemed to matter any more, and he sensed that it was because he had finally succeeded in his fight with HTR, for they would never recover from losing the trestle over the gorge.

'Put me on a wagon and sent me to Longhorn Crossing, Hank,' he told Belmont, 'and then get your crew back to end of track. There's still a lot of track to be laid.'

He closed his eyes and slipped back into the comforting blackness that was hovering around him, aware that the fighting was over and he would be able now to concentrate on aspects of life away from the railroad.